her sweet orc

love in whispering springs
book one

Meg Rhodes

EBook ISBN: 979-8-9907519-0-3

Paperback ISBN: 979-8-9907519-1-0

Developmental Editing - Sarah Daniels | @tormented.author.services

Line/Copy Editing- Quoth the Raven Editorial | @stephanievcanto

Formatting- Weaver Way Author Services | @weaverwayauthorservices

Cover Art - Kit Fox | @kitfoxart

This book is dedicated to myself. The younger version of me would be so proud of how far we've come, and how we made our dream come true.

It's never too late to heal and become your own hero.

content notice

This book is very sweet and funny, but there are some heavier topics discussed throughout. Mental health is incredibly important to me. Please be sure to read the content notice carefully so that you are able to take care of yourself. Also, please do not hesitate to reach out to me if you think that I missed something that should be included in the content notice. I'm human and make mistakes.

Email me at: megrhodesauthor@gmail.com

CONTENT NOTICE

Fatphobic comment by a rando douchebag not respecting personal space (on page, it's brief), vague possibility that said rando douchebag may have been harmed (not on page), mentions of adoption, mentions of previous partner's cheating (not MMC), parental/grandparent loss (not on page, but mentioned), anxiety rep, mentions of therapy, abandonment issues, struggles with grief, mentions of birth control, mentions of wanting to be a parent in the future, discussions about waiting to become pregnant

whispering springs

Welcome to Whispering Springs! Our quaint town is home to a delightful assortment of monsters and humans, who choose to call this little slice of heaven home. We are proud of Whispering Springs' place in history as the first town in the United States to welcome monsters and humans to live together in harmony. Whether you are looking to put down roots or visit one of our world-class small businesses, Whispering Springs is ready to welcome you with open arms.

Whispering Springs Chamber of Commerce

one
ada

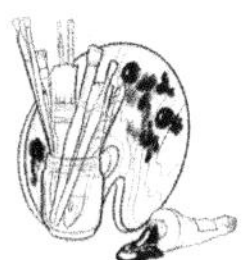

"Okay, okay, I'm getting up!" I groan, frustrated with my alarm for having the *audacity* to go off even though I was the one who set it.

Letting out a deep sigh, I allow myself a few more precious moments to enjoy the snuggly warmth of my bed. There are few things more satisfying than a comfortable bed first thing in the morning. Being wrapped up in my blanket burrito is my idea of a good time.

The peaceful moment doesn't last long, as my phone alerts me to a text message.

Seriously?

RUE

Remind me to never work the opening shift ever again. I'm going to need some serious caffeine so I don't rip the head off of every customer who comes into the shop today and asks stupid ass questions.

Customer service is certainly not Rue's strength. She's in rare form and the day has barely started. Rereading her message, I can't help but smile. I've never been a morning person, but Rue takes it to a whole other level.

My best friend must've been strong-armed by her equally strong-willed mother to take the early morning shift at her family's witch shop, The Enchantress. Rue comes from a long line of powerful and revered witches dating back centuries, and her coven has inhabited this area long before the town we live in was even founded.

ADA

Well good morning to you too, haha

Meet me for coffee at 8? Blissful Bites? We wouldn't want to subject the good people of Whispering Springs to your unique brand of early morning hostility.

RUE

If only you could see me flipping you off right now...

Blissful Bites, huh? This wouldn't have anything to do with the hunky orc owner that you've been drooling over, would it?

ADA

What?! I don't drool over him!

Okay, maybe just a little.

This is, of course, an enormous lie. Ulgan Durzum is the drop dead gorgeous baker and owner of Blissful Bites. The memory of the first time I saw him, just after moving to town a few months ago, is seared into my mind.

I went to the bakery to meet Rue for brunch, and stopped

dead in my tracks when I spotted him behind the counter. Over six feet of muscles, tattoos, and the most breathtaking deep green skin He also wears glasses, and hot nerds have always been my weakness. I've never dated anyone with tusks before, but I sure as hell am willing to give it a shot. It took Rue shouting my name to snap me out of my horny trance.

Definitely not my finest moment, but who could blame me? It's not every day you feel an instant, overwhelming attraction to someone. It sounds weird, but I almost swore there was some sort of magnetic pull to him.

RUE

Put cinnamon in your coffee today. You need some abundance in your life right now.

ADA

Abundance? Of what?

RUE

Orc dick… Get your head in the game, champ. It's time to fucking manifest yourself a boyfriend.

ADA

See you at 8.

RUE

Love ya

Shaking my head, I place my phone back on the nightstand. Maybe she's right. Not about the dick—though it would be a nice bonus—but about putting myself out there more. It's been almost a year since my last serious relationship, and *boy* did that crash and burn. After over two years, the douche lord cheated on me, then had the nerve to say it was my fault. He informed me he cheated because he felt I didn't trust him enough.

Gee, I wonder why?

The worst part is he wasn't even the first guy to fuck me over.

It's time to get back out there, even if the idea of dating makes me nauseous. My palms sweat just thinking about it. Why is it so hard to find someone these days? Is it too much to ask to meet a person that's kind, respectful, and loving?

All right, I've stalled long enough. It's time to get out of bed and get ready for work. The familiar voice of Dolly Parton filters into the room from the portable speaker in the corner. Singing off key, I twist my pale lavender hair into two space buns and can't help but smile. I've always wanted to dye my hair a fun color, but didn't have the confidence to do it until right before the move. It seemed like the perfect time to make the change.

Quickly changing out of my oversized tie dye shirt, I pull on a soft black and white striped t-shirt and a pair of worn-in denim overalls. They are covered in paint splotches. Most people probably would've thrown them away by now, but I believe the paint adds character, tells a story. Each drop of paint represented a memory or piece of art I created. Call me sentimental, but there's no way I'll ever part with them.

Standing in front of the full length mirror, confidence and self-love are evident in the reflection. It took a lot of healing to stop speaking negatively about myself and learn to appreciate my larger curvy body. To see the beauty in my soft stomach, strength in my thicker thighs, and a healthy appreciation for my fabulous ass. The woman staring back at me is deserving of respect and love, not only from others, but also from herself.

Swiftly grabbing my bag, I text Rue to let her know I'm on my way. It's time to go meet up with the chaos queen, and maybe dust off my flirting skills with a handsome orc while I'm at it.

two
ada

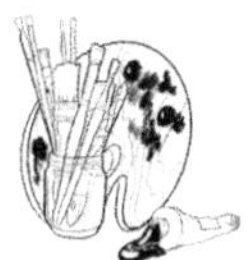

It's hard to put into words how much my friendship with Rue means to me. My parents died when I was just a little kid, and I was then raised by my incredible grandmother until she, too, passed when I was eighteen. I was alone again, until I met Rue.

She and her mother welcomed me, and always included me in family celebrations. The holidays had always been a depressing time of year for me until I started celebrating the Sabbats with Rue's coven. I still remember my first Yule, with the towering evergreen tree decorated with ornaments we handcrafted from dried orange slices and cinnamon sticks. I was made to feel like I was a part of the family, and it hasn't changed one bit. Whispering Springs became my new home, and I finally had the family I always craved.

It's almost comical how different my best friend and I are. Rue is fiery and outgoing, whereas I'm more of an introverted homebody. We met in Boston, where we both attended the same college and eventually became roommates. After graduation, she moved back to her hometown of Whispering Springs, Oregon, and I stayed in the city to live the life of a struggling artist.

It took her years to convince me to move here, but her persistence worked. Being hired as the new art teacher at the elementary school in town was the cherry on top of the sundae. It's time to plant roots and discover the sense of community that had been missing from my increasingly lonely life.

I spot Rue leaning against the brick exterior of Blissful Bites, scrolling through her phone. As if she can sense me, her head pops up and she walks over. A form fitting black jumpsuit hugs her curves, and one of her signature boho inspired kimonos flows in the wind. A perfect head of black curls fall around her shoulders.

I'm envious of how effortlessly cool she is. Rue's the real reason I learned to love my body. It's hard to speak negatively about yourself when you're friends with one of the most body positive women on the planet. She and I are similar in size, and she challenged me to try on her clothes in college to show me my body was worthy of being seen.

"What took you so long? I need coffee in my system ASAP. You know I get mean when I don't have my bean juice," Rue playfully whines.

Crossing the street, she and I link arms and enter the bakery. My senses are immediately overwhelmed with delicious scents. The rich aroma of coffee and sweet pastries never fails to put me in a good mood. I love small bakeries like this, where it's clear that it's a vital part of the town. I take in the familiar cream colored walls, many of which are covered in photos of customers at different community celebrations, or the Durzum family smiling while working side by side. To my left are a few white metal tables and chairs, all filled to the brim with people happily chatting. A large window at the front of the shop reveals the hustle and bustle of Main Street.

"Look who's behind the counter..." Rue whispers, wiggling her eyebrows at me. My heart quickens as I spot Ulgan. I swear, I never get tired of looking at him. Today, his powerful, hulking body is hidden under a plain blue t-shirt with a Blissful Bites apron on top. I could happily stare at his yummy muscular tattooed arms all day long.

"Good morning, ladies," he says, greeting us with his deliciously deep voice. Ulgan's warm chocolate eyes make my heart flip when they land on me before looking at Rue.

"Morning, Ulgan. We're here for the goods," Rue says.

He glances in my direction, giving me a warm smile which holds a touch of shyness. Ulgan nervously tucks a piece of his gorgeous straight black hair behind his ear that's fallen out of the bun he usually wears.

"Goods? Is that what we're calling your breakfast order now?" Ulgan replies with a chuckle. He hits me with that smile of his again and leans closer to me from across the counter. "Ada, why do you hang around this pain in the ass?"

Laughing, I reply, "Well, she's not always a pain in the ass. There are rare moments when she acts like a normal person and not a feral animal."

"Hey! I'm standing right here!" Rue places her hands on her hips in mock surprise at what we're saying.

Ulgan hands Rue her large black coffee and everything bagel. She greedily sips her coffee and lets out a loud groan. "My inner bitch has been satisfied."

"Well, I'm happy to hear it. Wouldn't want to anger her." Ulgan and I laugh. He turns to me and hands me my iced coffee and pumpkin muffin. His bigger hand brushes mine briefly before curling his fingers around my hand to hold it in place. His hand radiates delicious warmth. "What about you, Ada? What satisfies you?" Ulgan asks, the deep growly voice of his sending a shiver down my spine. His thumb gently traces circles across my palm. The light touch makes my core ache.

There is somewhere else, specifically between my legs, that I wouldn't mind that thumb to circle.

"Oh, um. Well." I'm completely tongue tied. Oh, I am *not* as smooth as I thought I'd be. Ulgan gives me a sensual smile.

Our eyes meet, and I swear the heat I see in those eyes reflects my own. My gaze briefly wanders to his lips, which look so damn soft and yummy. I've fantasized about them for months now. I wonder if those tusks of his are sensitive?

"Ada..." he says, his voice dropping an octave. Our little bubble is interrupted by a customer behind me clearing their throat, signaling that we've been standing here looking at each other for an embarrassingly long amount of time.

Ulgan pulls his hand back, reaching up to rub the back of his neck, his green cheeks darkening.

"I guess I should be going. Bye, Ulgan." I give him a shy smile and turn to leave. Rue must've left my side at some point, because she's now standing by the door.

"Um, Ada!" Uglan calls from behind me. I face him, and my heart skips a beat like it does every single time he says my name. "Same time tomorrow?" he asks, his arms crossing and uncrossing as if he's trying to figure out what to do with his hands.

Do I make him this nervous? The thought gives me a thrill.

"It's a date," I playfully reply.

Turning to face Rue, I scrunch my eyes closed. Did I really just say that? Please, universe, don't let Rue have heard. I finally reach her by the door, which she pushes open. Of course, not before Rue says, "It's a date," in a deep, sultry, mocking tone with an added shoulder shimmy.

"Oh, shut up," I reply and head outside. Rue and I make our way down Main Street, sipping our coffees. My iced latte tastes decadent with the rich mocha syrup.

Turning to Rue, I decide to tease my sweet friend. "Oh no, Rue, I forgot to ask for cinnamon in my coffee. I guess there won't be any abundance for me today." I chuckle.

Rue remains silent by my side, and I know exactly what it means. "You just used magic to put cinnamon in my coffee, didn't you?"

The smirk on her face and resounding silence speaks volumes.

Outside of Whispering Springs Elementary, it's time for us to go our separate ways. "Swing by my house after work?" I ask Rue.

"Will there be food? You know I don't go anywhere if there isn't food," she replies. I laugh. No one wants to see Rue when she hasn't eaten.

"Yes, the evening meal will be served promptly at six-thirty. Make sure you wear your finest attire to this culinary extravaganza," I reply in my awful English accent.

"Well, I would hate to disappoint the lady of the house," Rue plays along, giving me her best English accent that comes across as more Australian than English. "I shall be there, and as a token of my appreciation, I shall spare no expense and bring the finest bottle of Diet Coke that money can buy."

"My good lady, how truly generous of you! I must now take my leave of you to go shape the minds of this country's youth." I give her a deep curtsy.

"Fare thee well!" Rue calls as she continues down the street to open The Enchantress, and I enter the school, ready for a great day.

three
ulgan

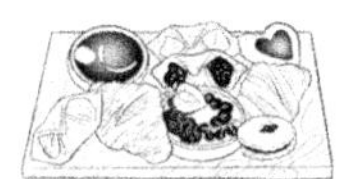

Watching Ada leave the shop every day is torture.

Our brief exchanges when she comes in to get her breakfast each morning aren't enough anymore, and to be honest, they never really were. Staring out the large glass window at the front of the shop, I find myself watching her until she disappears down the road.

"Ahem."

Crap, had I been that distracted? "Sorry, Mrs. Urqhart. I'll be right back with your tea."

Mrs. Urqhart is one of my regulars, and comes in each day for a cup of English breakfast tea with a splash of milk and two sugars. She's here for her usual order, so I quickly get to work brewing her tea. My mind floats back to Ada while I wait for the tea to steep. It took all of my self-restraint to not jump over the counter and pull her into my arms. Simply touching her hand has my head done in.

I'VE BEEN HIDING a secret for months now. As the days go by, it gets more and more difficult to keep it hidden. The first time I saw Ada, I knew she was my fated mate.

Her scent—calming lavender and vibrant lemon—hit me like a wall when she first entered the bakery. It's a scent I've looked forward to everyday since. Once orcs reach maturity at around sixteen, we are able to identify our mates through scent. It's something all young orcs hear stories about. Mom would tell my sister and I tales about the powerful pull fated mates feel toward one another. I'd almost given up hope that I would ever find my mate, and it still feels like a dream that she's here.

My soul calls for hers every minute of the day, and leaves an ache in my chest. It's become painful to be this close to the woman I'm meant to love with everything I am, but not feel that I'm able to claim her as mine.

Keeping this secret from my family and friends hasn't been easy. My mother suspects that something is up with me, but hasn't been able to figure it out just yet. Thankfully, my younger sister, Selene, is too busy with her new job in the city to be around much these days.

My childhood best friend, Theo, is another story entirely. The nosy elf knew instantly what was up, but took pity on me and didn't mention it. He does, however, enjoy teasing me about my lack of game.

I should have told Ada immediately when I figured it out, but the bitter fear of rejection kept me from going through with it.

Fuck. She's human, and I know humans don't experience the mating bond as orcs do. What if the idea of being tied to me for the rest of our lives terrifies her? I could lose her forever before I've even had her. It's been months now, and the few short minutes we interact with each other a day simply isn't enough anymore. I *need* more. More of her sweet smile. More of her adorable laugh. Last but not least, I need her sinful curves naked and in my bed.

I need more of everything when it comes to her.

Our easy banter this morning confirms what I already know. That gorgeous little human was made for me. What would it be like to wake up next to her every morning and share those small, daily moments together? I've spent more hours than I care to admit pining after Ada, and it's finally time for me to make her mine. I need to talk to Theo and see if he can help me figure out what to do.

A small part of me worries whether or not she'll forgive me for keeping this from her. Ada deserves to be wooed and spoiled, not forced into a lifetime commitment. I shoot a prayer to the Goddess that she's able to understand.

My mother comes through the double doors which lead to the back kitchen area, carrying a large tray of Halloween themed cupcakes. Each one was carefully decorated to look like either a jack-o'-lantern or witch's cauldron. Mom is a retired baker and the former owner of Blissful Bites until I bought the shop from her. She shows up sometimes to help when she misses being in the kitchen. I always look forward to her visits and let her have free reign. As the one who fostered my love of baking, I owe her everything and more for helping me realize my dream of owning this place.

"Hey, Mom. Are you okay here by yourself for a little while? I was going to head over to Theo's to see if he was free to grab lunch."

"Did you forget I ran this bakery for years without help? Go have some fun." She shoos me away with her hands. "You work too hard and deserve a break. While you're at it, maybe go on one of those dating apps, find yourself a nice woman to take out." When I don't respond, she narrows her eyes. "You have considered using the apps, haven't you?"

"*Mom.*" I take off my glasses to rub my eyes. "I'm not going to use any apps. You'll be happy to know there's actually someone I've been thinking about asking out, but we are not going to discuss it right now."

Her eyes light up. "There's someone you're going to ask out? Do I know her? What's her name?"

"Ma." I knew it was a bad idea to mention it to her.

"Right, right. I won't pry. Now, you get out of here. Take as much time as you need. It's slow right now and I'll be fine. Tell Theo I say hello."

I wrap an arm around her shoulders and pull her in to me, giving her a kiss on the head. "Thanks Mom. I love you. Call me if you need me." She starts to push me out the door before I can change my mind and try to stay.

Walking down the street I make my way to see the one person outside of my family that truly knows me.

Theo may be a cocky prick at times, but he's the best friend I've ever had. You'd think being larger than most of my classmates in school would've deterred them from picking on me, but as luck would have it, my size just added to their fun. Being nerdy and awkward certainly did not make me popular with girls. Thankfully, Theo was always there for me, and we continue to have each other's backs.

Pushing the door open to his antiques shop, Out of the Attic, my nerves start to get the better of me. What if this whole thing with Ada is just another way for the universe to fuck with me? I've always been anxious, and at times my anxiety is overwhelming.

The voice of my therapist plays in my mind during these times: "You are safe, and deserving of happiness. What you are feeling is only temporary." I've been seeing Dr. Mallory since I was in college to help with my mental health, and she hasn't steered me wrong yet.

I spot Theo with a heavy stack of books precariously balanced in his arms, walking over to the vintage book section. "Hey man, I'll be with you in just a second," he says with a grunt.

One thing I've always been envious of is how put together my friend is. Elves are known for their clean cut appearances, but Theo takes it to another level. All of his clothes are custom made, there isn't a hair out of place on his platinum blonde head, and his pointed ears always shine with a fair amount of golden earrings. I'm more of a jeans and t-shirt man, but I give Theo credit for having style.

"Need any help with those?" I offer, pointing to the books.

"Nah, I should be okay," he replies, placing the large pile on a nearby book cart. "Gotta keep my muscles in tip-top shape for the ladies."

"The ladies, huh?" I laugh.

"Well, we can't all be built like the Incredible Hulk, now can we?"

I roll my eyes in his direction and walk with him to the back of the shop where he keeps his office.

"Do you have a minute? I need to talk to you about something personal." This is harder than I thought it would be.

"Personal, huh? How personal are we talking? Because I'm not a doctor," he says with a smirk. I roll my eyes at his response. Theo's such a smartass.

"It has something to do with my future." Could I be any more vague? I just need to spit it out already.

"Does this have anything to do with the cute human that's your mate?" he asks, a shit eating grin on his face.

"What gave me away?" I'd suspected this, but to hear him say it out loud is another thing entirely. To hear anyone actually call her my mate is music to my ears. All of the anxiety leaves my body, and I relax into the chair in front of his desk.

"Well, either you've had a killer cold for months, *or* you've been scenting her. Also, you look like you're in physical pain each time she's around, like you're holding yourself back." Theo sounds concerned. "Has the mating heat hit yet? Because I would bet money that it has. You have all of the classic signs of an orc in heat."

"Yeah, it started months ago, but the suppressants I'm on make it almost bearable." Well, bearable might not be the best word to use. I crave Ada's presence all the time, and it does hurt to be away from her.

"I hate to break it to you, Ulgan, but you have a terrible poker face. You couldn't hide your feelings toward her even if you tried." His grin disappears, a gentle smile taking its place.

"What do I do?" I ask, desperate for his help.

Theo sits down in the seat opposite me. "I should think it's pretty obvious. You tell her and see what happens."

"Humans don't have mates. I could scare the shit out of her if I'm like, 'Oh hey, want to be bonded with me for the rest of your life?'"

"You're in your head too much. You need to get out of your own way." Theo leans back in his chair, crossing his legs at the ankle and resting his clasped hands on his stomach. “You don’t have to make some grand proclamation. Just ask her out on a date. A low key, casual date. Let her get to know you, and before you know it—BAM, you’ve got yourself a bonding ceremony to plan."

“Ask her out...I can do that.” My shoulders continue to relax and release their tension.

“Of course you can,” Theo says. “You wouldn’t be the first orc to mate with a human. I know this is new for you, but it’s nothing to worry about. Listen, you need to realize that you are a great guy who deserves to enjoy life with a wonderful little mate by your side.”

Now, this is why Theo is one of the best men I’ve been lucky enough to know. He’s always seen me for who I am.

Theo stands from his chair and grabs his jacket from a hook near the door. “There may just be someone who can help you. A certain witch with a bad attitude owes me a favor.”

If it’s who I think it is, I hope her inner bitch is still satisfied and in a charitable mood.

four
ada

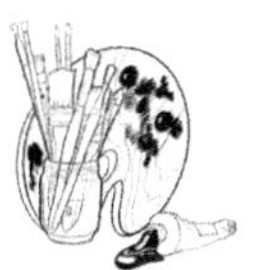

Working with kids has a way of humbling you.

No amount of experience or college classes will prepare you for the absolute chaos of elementary aged children. One moment you feel like you have everything under control, and the next you have a class of third graders throwing globs of clay at each other because it "seemed like fun." I spent my entire lunch period scraping chunks of thick wet clay off of the art room walls and tables.

The gym teacher would be proud, at least. Some of the kids really had good aim.

A cool breeze sweeps through the trees on my walk home from work, causing leaves in vibrant shades of red, orange, and yellow to dance around me. There's something transformative about this time of year. I wish I had my sketchbook and pencils with me to capture this serene moment.

Stopping at the small grocery store down the street from my house, I pick up all of the ingredients I'll need to make my favorite comfort meal: chicken and dumplings. The recipe was my Granny's, and it always helps me to feel closer to her whenever I make it. I really could use one of her warm hugs after the day I just had.

I finally make it home and close the door behind me, letting out a sigh of relief. Placing the groceries on the kitchen counter, I quickly change into comfy clothes and get to work on dinner. The comforting and familiar fragrance of the rich chicken and dumplings fill my house.

Rue walks in the front door just as I begin plating up our dinner. She and I are long past the days of ringing doorbells or knocking.

"Oh no, chicken and dumplings? What happened at work? Did the little demons not behave themselves?" she asks, taking a seat at the table.

"Rue, they're children, not demons," I reply, placing her plate down and taking my seat across from her.

"Yeah, well I beg to differ," she responds. At least she called them demons today instead of her typical *crotch goblins*.

"To be honest, demons might be the most accurate description for them today. Long story short, clay went flying everywhere. And I mean *everywhere*."

The chicken and dumplings are scorching hot, so I blow on it before taking a bite. Yep, Granny's recipes make everything better.

"Oh shit! That's rough, babe. Tomorrow will be better, and if it isn't, I can always make you a potion to force the little dears to behave." I laugh at her offer. She always knows how to make me feel better. She takes a bite of her food and her eyes dramatically roll back in her head. "Dammit, this is so good."

"How was work for you today?" I ask in between bites.

"As boring as ever. I keep trying to ask for more responsibility within the coven, but she denies me every time." The disappointment seeps through her words.

Rue has been trying to convince her mother, Angeline, to let her take on more of a leadership role. Each time she's told, *not just yet*, or, *when you're ready*. The tension this creates between the two of them can at times become explosive. Trust me, there is nothing more frightening than two pissed off witches.

Getting up from my chair, I cross the room and wrap her in a tight hug. She quickly returns it, and it's clear we both needed this.

We finish dinner and head to the living room to watch our favorite trash reality TV. Housewives behaving badly and warm chocolate chip cookies is exactly what we need right now.

"You won't believe who stopped by the shop today..." Rue trails off.

Pulling my attention from the show, I turn on the couch to face her. She tosses me a cookie before continuing.

"Theo and Ulgan."

My ears perk up at the mention of his name. I take a bite out of the cookie and wait for her to spill the tea.

"I may or may not have overheard your big green hunk mentioning how he wants to upgrade the bakery, and he's thinking about having an artist create a mural to liven the place up." Why does she have a weird grin on her face?

Suddenly, as if by magic, my phone alerts me of a new text message. Then it hits me like a ton of bricks. "You didn't." My voice filled with panic.

"Oh yes I did, my dear Ada. You can thank me later," Rue replies in an annoyingly musical tone.

UNKNOWN NUMBER

Hi Ada, it's Ulgan from Blissful Bites. Sorry to message you so late, but Rue mentioned that you might be able to help me with a project at the bakery.

I scream and throw my phone to her. She looks over the message and grins, tossing the phone back to me. Interfering witch!

"That's my cue to leave. Respond to him, babe. You don't want to keep your dream man waiting." She winks at me, grabs her coat, and leaves.

Glancing back at my phone, I pick it up and message him back. Play it cool, Ada!

ADA

Hi Ulgan! What kind of project did you have in mind?

ULGAN

The bakery hasn't been updated since my mom opened it back in the 90s. I was wondering if you might be interested in painting some art in the shop to bring some new life and color to it.

My imagination already goes wild with ideas for the space. Larger than life depictions of all of their yummy offerings and the ingredients used to make them would look perfect. I haven't had the time to do much art for myself recently, so this could be the perfect opportunity. Running into my bedroom, I grab my sketchbook and tools to put my ideas down on paper.

Before I can respond, another message comes through.

ULGAN

I loved the mural you created at the school over the summer. The town is lucky to have you.

My cheeks heat up, and a comforting warmth fills my chest. The mural at the school had been a labor of love. Each day, students visited me in the summer before school started to help me with different sections of the mural. It became a big community event, and the end result still brings a smile to my face each time I walk past it.

ADA

Thank you, I'm glad you like it. It was something I've always wanted to do, and I couldn't believe how wonderful the town was during the process. I would love to create something for the bakery!

ULGAN

That's awesome! Would you be available to do the artwork this weekend? I could mark off an area for you to work uninterrupted where the town can still see you work. You would have complete creative freedom, of course.

ADA

Not going to lie, I've already pulled my sketchbook out and have an idea, haha.

I take a picture and send it to him.

ULGAN

I knew you were talented, but it looks incredible. Ada, I really appreciate that you're doing this. When you get a chance, send me a list of supplies you'll need and I'll make sure that you have them. Also, how much do you usually charge for one of your murals? I'll pay you, of course.

ADA

Oh no, don't worry about it! I can take care of everything. No need to pay me.

ULGAN

Ada.

I can take care of everything that you will need.

Everything? My face begins to flush at his words.

ULGAN

Send over the list, Sunshine. Also, if you won't accept money for your time, will you accept baked goods and coffee?

Sunshine? My core clenches at that. It gives me a small thrill that he's chosen such an adorable nickname for me. Is he flirting with me right now?

ADA

Well, I never turn down coffee... You've got yourself a deal.

ULGAN

Great! I'll see you around 8 on Saturday?

ADA

I'll be there

ULGAN

Good night, Ada

I snuggle back down into the couch, hugging my phone to my chest. I'm probably making too big of a deal out of this, and it's all just a job. My happiness at hearing from him has now morphed into caution. Maybe Saturday will shed more light on the situation?

It certainly couldn't make me more confused. Right?

I pull the blanket off the back of the couch, and settle in to read before bed. A little late night smut always puts me in a better mood.

five
ada

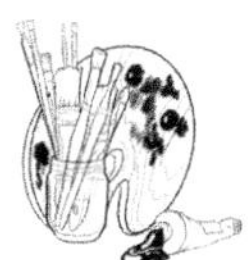

Thankfully, my week turns around by Friday, and the kids finally behave themselves. Today, they continue to work on their clay creations for the upcoming art night, and this time, the clay remains on the tables instead of the walls.

One of my students, Maisie, a pint-sized pixie, flutters over to me to show off the mug she made for her mother. "Ms. Walker, look what I made! I'm an artist, just like you." She beams up at me, holding out her creation. The mug was carefully crafted by her tiny hands, and it's clear she poured all of her love for her mother into it. "Do you think mama will like it?" she asks, sounding uncertain.

"Maisie, this might just be the most beautiful mug I've ever seen," I say. "You certainly are a fantastic artist, and your mother is going to love it, sweet girl."

She flashes me a toothless grin, having lost her two front teeth recently. The sweet pixie flitters back to her friends with a sense of pride that's clear in the way she carries herself. Moments like this make days like earlier this week worth it. Yes, there are days when I question my decision to become a teacher, but then moments like this happen and remind me of why I moved to Whispering Springs in the first place.

The only hiccup today was between an orc boy and a selkie girl. The poor little guy is still getting used to his growing body and accidently knocked over the little girl's project. After checking in with both of them, it was clear that it was an accident, and they ended up giving each other a hug and going off to fix her project together.

It has to be difficult to be a young orc trying to navigate a world that wasn't necessarily built to accommodate your larger stature. I wonder what it was like for Ulgan growing up. He must've been such an adorable child, with a lopsided grin and big kind eyes.

I'd be lying to myself if I said my heart doesn't ache to be a mother one day in the future. Though I didn't have my parents in my life for very long, Granny always made sure that I felt loved and special. She went to every parent-teacher conference, hosted every birthday, and taught me right from wrong. She showed me how to be a strong and kind hearted woman.

I hope to do the same for my children someday.

Three more classes later, I'm packing up my things and getting ready to head home when my phone buzzes. My breath hitches when I see a text from Ulgan. I open it and laugh. Taking up my screen is a photo of a smiling Ulgan standing in the bakery surrounded by the supplies I'll need for my project tomorrow.

This man is adorable without even knowing it. I thought it wasn't possible to be more attracted to him, but the universe decided to prove me wrong.

ULGAN

The space is all set for you tomorrow. Can't wait to watch you work your magic.

ADA

Magic, huh?

ULGAN

Everything about you is magical, Ada. I'll see you bright and early.

There was no mistaking his intentions this time. That beautiful orc is flirting with me. Tomorrow can't come soon enough.

A gentle knock on the door brings me right out of my daydreaming. "Sorry, Ada. I didn't mean to scare you." My coworker, Sarah, stands in the doorway to the art room. The wolf shifter was the first person who welcomed me to the school and made sure that I had everything I needed. She's been working in the school for a few years now, and has thankfully taken me under her wing.

"No, I'm the one who should be sorry. I was just thinking about something. Come on in."

Sarah makes her way into the art room and sits on top of one of the tables opposite me. "Who has you daydreaming and smiling like that?" she asks playfully.

My cheeks redden and a shy smile crosses my lips. "Just someone."

Her eyebrows shoot up in surprise. "A male someone?"

"Oh, a *very* male someone." Every single inch of Ulgan screams masculinity. "Do you have any plans this weekend?" I say, trying to change the subject.

"Max and I are staying at a cute B&B that we've been dying to visit. They're hosting a spooky murder-mystery themed party. You know how much I enjoy my true crime podcasts. There really is no way that we'll lose. How about you?"

"Well, my weekend isn't as exciting. There's a painting project on Saturday that I'll be working on, and then I'll relax on Sunday. I'm due for a good bath and face mask session." Okay, not the whole truth, but a little omission never hurt anyone, right?

She stands up from the table and her eyes soften. "Get out of here and go catch up on some well deserved relaxation. Have a great weekend!"

"You too. Go catch that murderer!" I wave goodbye before taking her advice and grabbing my bag to head home.

Walking through the halls of the school, I can't help but think back to my conversation with Sarah. I'm so envious of her relationship with her mate, and hope to one day have something like it for myself. What would it be like to come home to someone everyday? My mind is a jumbled mess of worry and apprehension about tomorrow. I need to take it easy on myself and really follow through with some self-care.

Near home, the plan for my evening is coming together. Tonight calls for a face mask, tacos, and the cinematic classic, *Raiders of the Lost Ark*.

six
ada

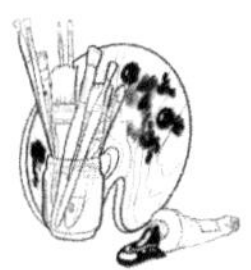

My alarm blares the next morning, butterflies already taking up residence in my stomach. No amount of Dolly Parton is going to calm me down today.

After taking way too long to get ready, I'm out the door and on my way to the bakery when I get a text from Rue.

RUE

Have fun today, and relax. You are a freaking badass and anyone would be lucky to be in your presence. You are a goddess and don't you forget it.
Love you!

Her message is just what I need. There's nothing like your best friend pumping you up to turn your mood around.

ADA

Love you! I'll text you tonight when I get home.

Fall is in full effect now, the wind picking up this morning and adding a bitter chill to the air. Thankfully, I remember to grab one of my old college sweatshirts before heading out the door. The worn material isn't the thickest thing on the planet, but at least it keeps me a bit warmer.

Stopping outside of Blissful Bites, I take a deep breath to steady myself. I need to remember that this is just a job that I've been hired to do. There's no reason for me to be this nervous. I'm Ada-freaking-Walker. Men should be nervous to be around me, not the other way around.

Taking another fortifying breath, I open the door wide and walk inside. It's early, so there are only a small handful of people waiting to place their orders. The bells above the door chime as I enter. Ulgan is busy chatting with a beautiful witch I recognize, Bea.

He spots me and waves me over. His adorable smile sucking me in again. "Good morning, Sunshine," he says.

This new nickname is doing things for me. I'm greedy and want to hear it again.

"Ada, have you met Bea? She and her partner Cassidy belong to Rue's coven."

"Hi, Bea. Yeah, we've met before. Though I had no idea you and Cassidy were together." How have I not noticed before?

"Really? Yeah, she and I have been seeing each other for about a decade."

"A decade?" I knew witches had the ability to slow down the aging process, but... "Bea, don't take this the wrong way, but how old are you? You don't look a day over twenty-five"

"Wouldn't you like to know." She winks. "Let's just say, I wasn't born in this century. Wait until I tell Cassidy you thought I was twenty-five. She's going to get a kick out of that." We all laugh.

"I have to get going, but how about the four of us grab dinner sometime?"

Before I can answer, Ulgan does for me, "We'd love to. Text me."

I stare at him, and he gives me a shy smile. Bea leaves and he turns to me. "Sorry about that. I should have asked you before accepting. Guess I just got a little excited."

"Excited about what?"

"The idea of having dinner with you." He avoids making eye contact as he clears his throat.

"Hypothetically speaking, if you were to ask me to dinner, I would say yes."

"Hypothetically speaking," he repeats and meets my gaze, humor evident in his voice.

"Purely hypothetical." I don't know what comes over me, but I place my hand on his forearm. There is this overwhelming need to touch and comfort him. He places his much larger hand over mine, curling his fingers around my hand to hold it there.

Without letting go, he leads me over to the large blank wall that I'll be painting today. A table nearby is filled with paint brushes, rollers, and various cans of paint. There's something about new art supplies that brings me an unbelievable amount of joy.

"I hope I ordered the right stuff." Ulgan gestures to the supplies, which are *way* more than I asked for. He must've spent a small fortune on all of this. Everything is top of the line.

"This is perfect!" I run my fingers over the soft paint bristles. My plans for the mural flood my brain, and I almost forget that he's still standing right next to me.

"I'm going to assume by your far off look that I've done good," he teases.

"Oh, you've done very well." I want to throw myself at him and show him just how well he *really* did. I decide climbing him like a tree in the middle of his business is probably not socially acceptable, and settle for a quick but satisfying hug.

It's time for me to get to work.

Ulgan returns my all too brief hug before I take a step back to admire the supplies again. "Let me know if you need anything at all. I'm just going to be over there." Ulgan points to the counter. "At the counter. Which is over there."

Is he nervous too?

I grab his hand, holding it in mine. The fact that he's just as nervous as me gives me a boost of confidence. "Thank you for asking me to do this. It's going to be so much fun to create this for you."

"You were the first person I thought of. I'm glad that you agreed. It'll be nice to get to know you better." He looks like he has more to say as his mouth opens and shuts like a fish out of water, but just then, customers come in that he needs to tend to.

After sketching a rough outline of my design, it's finally time to paint. Unfortunately, my short legs can't reach high enough on the wall to paint the top half of the design, so I have to climb onto the ladder that Ulgan set up. Everything is going smoothly, until I move the wrong way and lose my balance, falling backwards.

My body tenses up, preparing to hit the hard floor when thick arms corded with muscle catch me, and I'm cradled to a warm and equally muscular chest. Looking over at my rescuer, I'm now inches away from Ulgan's face. How did he get over here so fast?

"Ada, are you alright?" he asks, scanning my body for injuries.

Absent-mindedly, I snuggle closer to him. "I'm okay, just a little shaken up."

He continues to hold me in his arms, tightening them around

me. Ulgan silently studies my face, and I avert my eyes, feeling overwhelmed by the attention.

His palm comes up to cup my right cheek. "Do you have any idea how beautiful you are?" He begins to lean in toward me, and my heart beats an unsteady rhythm because I know what's coming next. Or at least, I sure as hell hope I know what's going to happen next.

His warm breath fans across my face, and I find myself mesmerized by the lust reflected back at me in his eyes. Our lips are drawn together like magnets and almost touch.

The bell to the front door sounds.

We instantly put distance between ourselves, and he places me back down on the ground. I could've sworn that I heard a low growl of frustration come from him.

Holy crap! Did that seriously just happen? Well, that's an interesting development.

"Good afternoon, Ms. Walker. Ulgan. I hope we aren't interrupting anything," a voice says from the doorway. Ulgan runs his palm over his face, and his signature smile returns as he chats and helps the elderly minotaur couple who just walked in.

Before I step back on the ladder, I can feel Ulgan's presence behind me, his breath heating the back of my neck. A growly deep voice whispers in my ear, "We are not finished." His heat disappears, and I finally release the breath I'd been holding in.

This orc is going to be the death of me.

Climbing back up the ladder, I get back to painting. The larger than life depictions of pastries and desserts add color and whimsy to the space. I pop my headphones on and find myself bobbing my head to the beat. Music always gets me in a creative headspace.

After about an hour, Ulgan taps on my shoulder. "It's coming along great, Sunshine."

His compliment washes over me. "Thanks, I'm glad that you like it so far."

"Would this be a good time for a break? I was thinking about closing up the shop for a bit so we could walk over to the park to enjoy the sun and have lunch." It's then I notice the blanket and wicker picnic basket in his hands.

"You just so happened to have a picnic basket ready to go?" I tease.

"A little too eager?" he asks. "One of my closest friends told me I needed to start going after what I want."

"And what is it that you want?" When did I get so bold? Get it, girl!

"You. I want to get to know you, Ada. I'm sorry it's taken me this long to do something about it." He reaches out and takes my hand, giving it a squeeze. "Is this something that you'd want to explore with me? I completely understand if you aren't interested. I won't pressure you into anything, but I just needed for you to know..." Ulgan is rambling, and I can see the panic setting in.

Be brave, Ada. Gently tugging on the front of his t-shirt, I press my lips to his.

The kiss starts out gentle at first, and I begin to worry that I overstepped and shouldn't have crossed this line. Ulgan's body is rigid, and I start to pull back. Just when I think I'm going to have to run out of here, he releases a heavy moan and the picnic basket is dropped to the ground with an audible *thud*. He wraps his powerful arms around my back like two steel bands.

It's official—I'm a big fan of tusks. His rest on my face and take a little getting used to, but they're so very *him*. I pull back, and a brilliant smile spread across his lips.

One final quick peck, and he pulls back further, but doesn't let go. "Goddess, Ada. Feel free to shut me up like that any time you want." I giggle, and he rests his forehead on mine so we're eye to eye. "So, about that picnic..." He pulls his face away, leans in and kisses my forehead briefly.

Forehead kisses are elite. There is nothing sweeter, and no one can prove me wrong.

"I'm not going to lie to you, I'm starving."

"If it's food my girl wants, it's food she's going to get."

His girl. I like the sound of that.

seven
ulgan

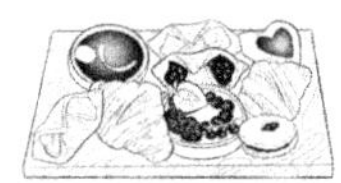

Am I dreaming right now? The other day I was sitting with Theo worrying that Ada wouldn't want anything to do with me, and now the woman of my dreams is holding my hand as we get ready for our first date.

This is a date, right?

I put way too much pressure on myself. I need to spend more time enjoying what's happening right now instead of worrying about the future. I'm going to take in this moment.

Ada and I make the short walk to the park, passing others who have also chosen to take advantage of the unexpected warm weather.

"I brought a few drinks for us," I say, "but I figured it might be fun to grab food from one of the food trucks."

"I love a good food truck. Which one is your favorite?"

"Well, it depends on what you're in the mood for. Pizza or sandwich?"

"Sandwich."

"I'm on it. Do you want to set up the blanket while I go get the food?"

"Sounds good to me," Ada says, and gives me the gift of her sweet laughter.

I return a little while later, and it's almost shocking how comfortable we are together. We share stories about our childhoods, who our quirky friends are, and our mutual love of *Indiana Jones* movies.

After we finish eating, we walk around the park, continuing to get to know each other. According to my mate, her favorite color is sky blue, the ocean is where she feels most at peace, and her dream is to own a house with a big front porch so that she can look at the stars at night. Each new piece of information that I learn about her feels like a new piece to the puzzle that is Ada Walker, and I find myself greedy for more. I find myself trying to commit every bit to memory.

"So you mentioned that you have a sister. Are you two close?" she asks, her shoulder brushing against mine. It shouldn't thrill me, but it does.

You'd think I'd never been around a woman before.

"Yeah, Selene and I were incredibly close growing up, and still talk all the time even though she lives a couple thousand miles away for work." It sucks that my younger sister Selene and I live so far from each other. My mom always jokes that she waited for us to wake up one day and not be able to stand each other, but that day never came.

"What does your sister do?" Ada asks, sincerely interested.

"She's an event planner for this big entertainment company. You should see the parties she puts together. They're absolutely insane." I envy my sister's ability to bring her visions to life.

"She has such a cool job. You really love your sister, huh?"

"Yeah, she's all right." I give Ada a wink to indicate that I'm joking with her.

"So, I know about your sister, but what about your mom and dad?"

I can feel myself grinning thinking about the story of how Selene and I came to be with our mom.

"Well, it's kind of a long story, but Selene and I were adopted by our mom when we were young. Even though her mate had died recently, she didn't hesitate to drive all night to pick us up when she received a call one day that two orclings had been abandoned and needed a home. Our family isn't conventional, but I wouldn't change a single thing about it."

My mother has always been a remarkable woman to me. She rescued and raised two orclings by herself while running a bakery, and while always staying present for Selene and I.

"Your mother sounds wonderful," Ada says.

My mother would also think that you *are wonderful,* I think, but I'm not weird enough to voice it out loud.

"She is." Edie Durzum is a force to be reckoned with. "Would you like to stop for some ice cream before we head back?" As much as I enjoy ice cream, this is really just a desperate attempt to spend more time with Ada.

"It's always a yes from me when ice cream is involved!" Ada's eyes sparkle at the mention of the chilly treat.

Her enthusiasm makes me chuckle. We walk over to the ice cream shop that's across the street from the park. Ice cream is one of my weaknesses, and I have it more times a week than I should. Ada orders a scoop of blueberry cobbler ice cream and I go with my favorite, mint chocolate chip. After some playful teasing from Ada about ordering "frozen toothpaste," we sit on a bench outside of the shop to enjoy our dessert.

Watching Ada's little pink tongue lap at her ice cream is a sensual experience. What I wouldn't give to see what else her tongue can do. Ada sinfully runs her tongue around the top of the cone, and then her eyes close as she gives a satisfied moan which sends a jolt straight to my cock. Images of Ada's tongue lapping at my length just like her damn ice cream instantly arouses me.

Shit, I need to stop thinking like this or else I'll scare her with a massive hard on. All right Ulgan, think about the least sexy things you possibly can; global warming, sad dog videos, people who use the word 'bae', sauerkraut... This seems to be working.

Glancing at Ada, she is now licking melted ice cream off of her finger.

I'm screwed.

We fortunately finish our ice cream before the threat of another erection, but unfortunately, we make our return to the bakery. Man, it was hard to leave the park. This was the best date I've ever been on, and the idea of it ending makes me wish we could do this everyday.

We work for a few more hours, chatting and listening to music over the bakery's speakers. Eventually, Ada comes bouncing over to the counter to tell me the mural is ready for me to see.

"All right, handsome, I'm going to need you to close your eyes for the grand reveal." It pleases me beyond belief that she thinks I'm handsome. Her small hands are on my back now as she leads me over to the wall. It makes me crave more of her touch.

"Okay, are you ready?" Her excitement is evident in each and every word.

"Yes, Sunshine. I'm ready," I respond with a light chuckle.

"You can open your eyes in 3, 2, 1!" she energetically shouts.

Lowering my hands from my face, all of the breath leaves my body as I gaze at her work. How the hell did she capture this bakery, this town, so well? My recipes were brought to life and immortalized forever. The mural is bursting with vibrant colors that immediately draw you in and capture your attention. Massive cupcakes, cookies, pies, and croissants fill the space and look shockingly realistic.

"Ada, I don't know what to say." I stare, transfixed on the vibrant work of art.

"Do you like it?" she asks, sounding unsure of herself. We can't have that now.

"Like it? I love it! Sunshine, you truly have a gift." Picking Ada up off the floor, I pull her into a hug. Her giggle is music to my ears.

She wraps her arms around me. "Okay, you had me worried there for a second."

I hate to do it, but I place her back on the ground.

Theo was right, I put too much pressure on myself to win Ada over when all I need to do is be myself.

The sun setting outside lets me know that it's time to close the bakery for the day. Ada asks if she can help me with the final preparations for the next day, and I'm struck by how natural this feels. Having her with me, laughing together as we get work done. I leave the rest of the prep for my baking assistant, Benji. He's helped take a lot of the load off of my shoulders recently, and I'm lucky to have him.

We close up the shop, and I'm thankful that Ada takes me up on my offer to walk her home. Hopefully she can't see it for what it is: my desperate attempt to spend even just a few more moments with her.

Her thin sweatshirt isn't a match for the chill in the air

tonight. I wrap my arm around her shoulders, pulling her into my warmth. A goofy grin spreads across my face as she snuggles into my side.

The walk to her house is far too short, and I can't help but wish that we had more time. This woman has wrecked me for anyone else.

"Thank you for walking me home." A shy smile and stunning ocean eyes gaze back at me. "I had a really fun time today, Ulgan."

"I did too, Sunshine."

Ada lets out a little laugh. "Is that my nickname now?" she asks.

"You are a ray of sunshine, so the name fits," I say, shrugging one of my shoulders. I omit the fact that I'm desperate for her sunshine in my life on a more permanent basis. The fates truly found me my perfect mate. "I'd love to get to know you more. Would you like to go out again? With me." Fuck, could I be any more awkward?

"I would love to," she says, moving in closer to me.

"Ada, I really want to kiss you right now," I blurt out.

She gives a soft chuckle, angling her head upwards. "Do you see me stopping you?" she replies with an amused grin.

I bend down and press my lips to hers, keeping the pressure gentle. A small sigh leaves her lips, and the sound is a balm to my soul. Being this close to her scent, I feel at peace.

My lips leave hers, and she gives my hand a gentle squeeze. I'm starving for her touch now, but I can't rush this. "Goodnight, Ulgan."

"Goodnight, Sunshine."

Ada walks into her cottage, and I wait for the door to close before walking back down the path and back to my apartment above the bakery.

I don't like the idea of spending another night alone in my bed, but hopefully I won't be alone for much longer. My mind wanders, wondering what it'd be like to wake up each morning with a naked Ada laying next to me. Her sleepy eyes settling on me, and being able to hold her or sink my cock deep into her body.

This train of thought needs to stop or I'll be walking around town with a massive hard on.

Yeah, if today was just a glimpse of what my life would be like with Ada in it, then I need more of my sunshine.

eight
ada

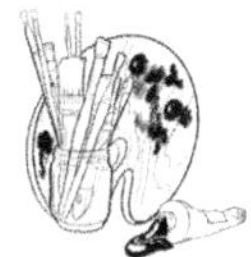

I've always been a bit of a loner. Making friends was never easy for me when I was growing up, so I developed a deep and devoted friendship with books instead. There were countless hours spent under the covers reading about far away lands, action packed quests, and true friendship that stood the test of time. Books became my lifeline when the world around me became too overwhelming.

It wasn't until I began staying with Rue and her mom in Whispering Springs during holiday breaks that I started to find and build the friendships that I'd always craved.

Hannah was the first friend I made on my own in town. She's one of the few humans who lives in Whispering Springs, and we bonded over our humanness almost immediately. Well, it also was our love of monster smut. Hannah is a librarian at the town library and is one of the most genuinely kind people I've met. She's always ready with a kind word and willing to listen. She's the human embodiment of a warm hug.

The newest member to my little friend group is Isla. She's the first dragon shifter I've ever met, and I'm still embarrassed about the first time we interacted. Isla, her daughter, and mother had been at the library a few months ago checking out books. I'd been carrying my usual pile of books to check out, the stack so high that it obscured my view. Unfortunately, my lack of sight led me to run poor Isla over, knocking her to the ground.

My books flew in every direction, thankfully missing her. I'd been terrified of seriously hurting her, profusely apologizing. But in typical Isla fashion, she dusted herself off while laughing, and complimented my taste in books as she helped me pick them up. Her mother and daughter joined us shortly after and the four of us went for ice cream, my treat of course. It was the least I could do for assaulting her with heavy hardcovers.

Female friendships tend to get overlooked, but there is such magic in finding a group of weirdos who love and accept each other's unique brand of weirdness. That isolating sense of loneliness is something of the past. It also helps that each of my friends is curvy, just like me. Being surrounded by strong, kickass fat women has empowered me like nothing else. I'm so thankful for them.

I should probably stop being sentimental and get started on dinner since it's my turn to host Girls' Dinner—a big freaking pasta dinner. Was I a bit of an overachiever by making three different pasta dishes? Absolutely. Should every pasta dinner include fettuccine alfredo, penne alla vodka, and shrimp scampi? Duh. The girls were bringing the sides and drinks, so thankfully I didn't need to worry about that.

A sudden knock at the door makes me pause. It's not time yet, is it? "I'm coming!" I shout, strolling to the door and yanking it open. My eyes widen to the size of dinner plates with surprise to see the sexy orc who is on the other side.

"Ulgan, I wasn't expecting you!" I exclaim. The butterflies in my stomach erupt into a happy dance. Well, my night just got way better. Ulgan's muscular frame fills my doorway, and I can't help but check him out. It should be illegal for someone to look this hot all the time. His jeans, t-shirt, and open flannel button down make him look like a sexy lumberjack.

Nervous energy radiates off of his body as he rubs the back of his neck and shifts from side to side. "You mentioned yesterday at lunch that you and your friends were having dinner together tonight, and I thought you might like some fresh bread to go with it," he says, holding out a massive crusty loaf of bread. It must be fresh out of the oven, because it's still warm and smells heavenly.

"Thank you, Ulgan. Bread is the way to every woman's heart. This is so thoughtful of you. Would you like to come inside for a minute?" I step aside so that he can enter.

"I wish I could, but I'm meeting up with some of my buddies tonight," he says, shaking his head regretfully. "Maybe another night?" He's so hopeful it nearly hurts.

"Of course." I flash him my best flirty smile, hoping it actually looks flirty rather than crazed.

"I better get going. Have a great night, Ada. I'll text you," he says. Appearing more confident now, he leans over and places a kiss on my cheek. His smooth lower tusks brush against my soft skin, and I like it way more than I care to admit.

I might be imagining things, but did he just sniff me? I'm not judging or anything, since I find myself taking a whiff of his cologne each time he's near me. The big guy always smells like a mouthwatering combination of pine and spice.

We wave to each other as he stands at the end of the path leading to my house before he heads up the street, hands in his jeans pockets, with a noticeable spring in his step. Each time I think he couldn't get any more adorable, he goes and proves me wrong. I scold the butterflies moshing in my stomach to calm down, and get back to work on dinner.

Thirty minutes later, Rue, Hannah, and Isla surround my small kitchen table with their plates piled high. Our weekly dinners may seem like a small thing to others, but I've come to look forward to these days each week. Since I have no family of my own anymore, these girls have become my family, and I try to soak up every moment I can get with them.

"All right, who has some tea to spill? I need hot gossip to liven up this boring week," Hannah says through a mouthful of pasta. All manners go out the window when we're all together.

"Wait, ladies, haven't you heard? Our dear Ada has an admirer that's dying to get in her pants," Rue coyly shares with everyone.

I shoot her a warning glare, my eyes narrowing, wishing that she would be quiet. It's hard to explain, but talking about my love life makes me uncomfortable. I've always had bad luck with dating, so it's hard to be excited about getting to know someone new when every other time I've done the same thing, I end up beating myself up and crying on my best friend's couch.

"WHAT? You've been holding out on us," Hannah exclaims, a smug grin forming and her eyes widening. "Who is it? Have we met him? Does he live in town? Spill, girl!"

This is the most animated I've seen Hannah in a long time. She hasn't been this excited since she learned Ruby Dixon was coming to the next town over for a book signing and we got to meet her. Our usually-calm Hannah became an unhinged fangirl.

Isla's musical laughter fills the room. "Does it rhyme with 'schmulgan' by any chance?" The smug dragon was going to pay for this later. Rue must've spilled the beans. Those two are now at the top of my shit list.

"Ulgan!" Hannah screams with glee, bouncing in her seat. "Holy crap, he's such a cinnamon roll!" A dreamy look filters across her face. She begins dramatically fanning herself with her hand.

"Um, honey, the guy is an orc, not a pastry. He does look awfully sweet though," Isla replies, patting Hannah on the hand. Clearly she doesn't understand what Hannah is talking about.

"No, even though I completely agree. A cinnamon roll is a character in a romance novel, usually one of the main characters, who's a complete sweetheart. They're kind, supportive, and treat their love interest like gold," Hannah explains.

"Thank you, Miss Librarian, for teaching us something new today," Rue says playfully.

Suddenly, a piece of bread flies across the table, bouncing off Rue's head. Everyone bursts into laughter as Hannah gets up to kiss Rue on the head as a peace offering.

"Ada, tell us more about Ulgan. Have you guys gone out yet?" Isla asks.

"Well, he asked me to help add some art to the bakery, thanks to a certain meddling witch." I narrow my gaze at Rue, who is now pretending to inspect my ceiling instead of making eye contact with me. "There's not much to tell just yet. We're getting to know each other, but he did take me out for a picnic yesterday in the park."

"How did it go?" Hannah probes.

I don't want to gush or get my hopes up, so I try my best to keep my cool. "It went well. He's a really great guy, and I want to continue getting to know him." Dammit, I hope I was convincing enough.

Rue's eyes examine my face, and I know that I can't hide anything from her. She knows about my dating past and how it's been difficult for me to trust men after being burned so many times. Opening up to new people is something I've been working on.

"I think it's wonderful that you're putting yourself out there like this. Dating is supposed to be fun, so enjoy getting to know him. You deserve to be with someone who recognizes how incredible you are." Isla says, reaching across the table to give my hand a comforting squeeze.

Hannah gives me a thoughtful look. "He would be one lucky guy to get our Ada."

I love these women so damn much. They know just what to say.

Rue stands up from the table. "All right ladies, it seems like all of us could use a night of drinking, dancing, and making poor life choices. How about we go and take a little field trip to The Wolf's Den?"

nine
ada

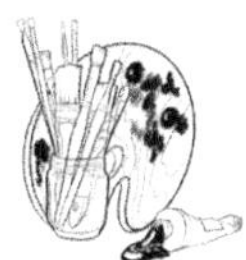

"I'm in. It's been way too long since I've let loose and had some fun," Hannah chimes, shimmying in her seat. Hannah looks like she's all sweet and shy, but she has a wild side.

Isla sits quietly across from me, and it's obvious she's trying to decide if she wants to go or head home to her daughter. I whisper to her, "Hey, don't feel pressured to go with us. But—and this is a big but—I would love it if you came out, even just for a little bit."

I can see her thinking through what I said, and moments later she addresses the table. "I'm in, too. Just let me text my mom to make sure she's okay with watching Kaida longer."

We all cheer, as she laughs, sending a quick text. Within seconds, she has her response and we're all filing out the door. The dishes can wait until tomorrow. I've never had a group of girlfriends like this, and I'm so thankful to have found them. We giggle like teenagers as we walk the few short blocks to The Wolf's Den, the pub in town.

Rue told me about The Den, as it's called by locals, back when we were in college. It's owned and run by the wolf shifter pack who live on the outskirts of Whispering Springs, preferring their privacy and freedom. The pub is known for its loud music and lively customers, who can be a bit rough around the edges at times.

We arrive at the pub, overflowing with humans and monsters of all kinds. A live band plays in the far corner surrounded by couples dancing along. The bar is filled with bodies, packed tight together, so we decide to sit at one of the free booths which line the side of the space. The worn leather of the booth feels smooth against my fingers as I take a seat.

Our waitress, a woman around our age, comes over to take our order. She looks familiar, but I don't think we've ever met. "Hi ladies! Welcome to The Den. My name's Clio and I'll be taking care of you." Her eyes land on me, and she tilts her head to the right, looking at me. "Okay, this is a long shot, but is your name Ada by any chance?"

"Yes, I'm Ada. Have we met before? You look so familiar," I say, my brows dip.

"No, we haven't met before, but I've heard about you from my aunt, Sarah. You work with her, right? She was telling me the other day about her work friend Ada, and you fit her description. Love the purple hair, by the way."

That's why she looks so familiar to me! She has the same curly red hair and striking golden eyes as Sarah.

"Sarah was telling me a few weeks ago how you just moved to the area recently. It's so nice to meet you." Turning to everyone at the table, I go around introducing Rue, Isla, and Hannah. "Wait, you're Sarah's niece? You couldn't be more than a year or two younger than her."

"Yeah, we get that a lot actually." Clio laughs. "My mom and Sarah's mom, my grandmother, were pregnant a year apart from each other. Sarah was the surprise 'later in life' baby. She and I weren't raised together, but reconnected once I made the decision to move here. Now we're inseparable."

"It's awesome to meet all of you. Everyone's first round is on me." Clio smiles at everyone at the table.

Clio seems like a sweetheart. I should invite her and Sarah to my place next week for a girls' dinner. It would be good for our little group of women to grow.

"What can I get you all?" Rue, Hannah, and Isla order their usual drinks. Clio's gaze falls on me.

"I'm feeling adventurous tonight. I'll have whatever your favorite mocktail is on the menu." The taste of alcohol has always been unappealing to me, so I've become a mocktail expert.

Clio chuckles. "Oh, I have just the thing for you. It isn't on the menu, but I think you'll love it. One mystery mocktail coming right up!"

Hurrying over to the bar, Clio hands our order off to the bartender, who I now notice is staring intensely at Isla. The man behind the counter is easily over six feet tall with golden skin deliciously covered in tattoos. His dark hair is beginning to gray around the temples, giving him a yummy older man vibe. His features are sharp and defined, and the five o'clock shadow is just the icing on the hunky cake.

"Rue," I whisper to her, "who's the bartender?"

She looks over my head and whispers back. "That's Sebastian, he's the alpha of the Artemis Pack. He's got the whole sexy brooding and growling thing down. Why do you ask? I thought you only had eyes for your big green dude?"

I poke her in her side. "I'm not asking for me, I'm asking for Isla. Look, he can't take his eyes off her. Don't say anything though, I don't want to spook her."

She looks over to him again and slowly slides back down in her seat. "Damn, I think I just got second hand eye-fucked." She dramatically fans herself. We laugh and rejoin the conversation the girls are having.

Our drinks arrive, and Clio places the most elaborate mocktail I've ever seen in front of me. The tall chilled glass is filled with a gorgeous blue liquid with a slight shimmer to it.

"Now, it's time for the magic to happen," Clio announces as she pours a small glass of what appears to be lemonade into my drink. Before my eyes, my glass becomes a sparkling galaxy, as the blue liquid slowly turns purple. Wait, are those ice cubes shaped like mini spaceships?

"I like to call this drink, *Sex on a Spaceship*," Clio says proudly. "I'm a huge fan of alien romance books. It's made with butterfly pea flower tea, lemonade, club soda, and edible glitter. It's got this whole galaxy vibe. Have a sip and tell me what you think."

I raise the chilled glass to my lips and take a drink. My taste buds are dancing right now. The tart lemonade perfectly balances out the bitter earthy tea.

"Holy shit, it's incredible!" Everyone at the table laughs, and Clio joins in. "Also, the name is perfection." Yeah, I am absolutely inviting Sarah and Clio for dinner. Clio and Hannah are going to get along *very* well.

Clio leaves us to tend to other tables, and before I know it, Isla and I are being dragged by Hannah and Rue over to the makeshift dance floor. The music blares through the speakers and the four of us sway to the beat, singing along off-key. This is exactly the night I needed.

The next song begins and it's just as upbeat as the last. I'm in my own world, just feeling the music when a pair of hands grab my hips in a tight, almost painful grip.

I whirl around and see that the offending hands belong to a man who gives off negative energy, making me immediately uncomfortable. "Hey sexy, come dance with me," he demands, a sleazy smile on his stupid face.

Pushing my hands against his chest to give me some space, my blood begins to boil. How dare this asshole try to ruin my good night. I refuse to give him a reason for not wanting to dance with him. I just give him a simple and firm, "No."

Mr. No One Tells Me No doesn't appear to take kindly to my rejection and attempts to paw at me again. His face shifts to one of anger, and something darker lurking just beneath the surface. "Do you know how lucky you are that I even asked you to dance, you fat slut?" he spits venom in each and every word.

"What the hell did you just call her?" a deep voice growls behind me. A second later, Ulgan is there, standing between me and the man.

"Mind your own business, you monster freak," the man who clearly has no self-preservation skills shouts at a hulking orc.

Ulgan's nostrils flare and lips tighten, his face fills with rage. His usually kind eyes darken as he edges closer to the source of probably everyone in this place's frustrations.

A well-dressed man with a slender build and long platinum hair grips Ulgan by the shoulder. Wait a minute, are those pointy ears? This must be his friend Theo that he told me about. I'd only ever seen him at a distance before, so this is one hell of a way to meet.

"Ulgan, he's not worth it. Let Sebastian and his pack handle him." Instantly, the bartender Sebastian appears next to me, flanked by two equally muscular men.

Sebastian tips his head toward the grabby asshole and his men walk over, grip him forcefully under each of his arms, and escort him kicking and screaming from the building like an upset toddler.

"No one disrespects women at The Den. Have some fucking pride, man. Quit acting like a pup!" Sebastian's gravely voice shouts. "Are you okay, sweetheart? My name is Sebastian, and this is my place," he says with a hint of a southern accent, looking me over. A growl comes from behind me.

Was that Ulgan?

"Meant nothing by it, old friend," he says, lightly smacking Ulgan on the shoulder. Did I miss something? What is he apologizing for?

The two men with Sebastian return, one of them whispering in his ear. He nods to them and they disappear through the crowd. The alpha turns toward Ulgan and me. "The situation has been taken care of. That piece of shit will never bother you again."

"When you say 'taken care of,' do you mean banned from this place, or—"

"Do you really want to know?" he asks, raising an eyebrow.

"Nope. I'm good with not knowing." I've watched enough true crime shows to know not to question a man who could potentially have a man killed just now. I'm not going to jail for being an accomplice. "Thank you, Sebastian."

Sebastian strolls away from us and takes his place back behind the bar.

"Ada, are you alright? Did he hurt you?" Ulgan asks, giving me his own once over. His earlier fury is still smoldering.

Rue appears next to me. "Where the fuck is that prick?" she shouts. "I'm going to curse his stupid ass so his dick shrivels up and falls off!" Pure rage fills her voice.

"Damn, little witch. You'd go after his dick?" Theo smirks and gives a hearty chuckle.

"I told you, don't call me that, or else it will be your dick I go after," she replies, and it becomes evident that Rue realizes what she just said as her eyes widen in shock.

"You can go after my dick whenever you want, Blackwood," Theo playfully quips. Rue, for the first time since I met her, is actually speechless.

Her eyes narrow at him, and she finally finds her voice. "You seriously never change. You're the same ridiculous prick that you were in high school. Some of us have evolved, you know?" She holds her chin high and rolls her eyes at him.

"Ada?" Ulgan asks, sounding unsure and bringing my attention back to him.

Rue is on a warpath wanting to destroy the asshole who may or may not be in this world anymore. I just don't have the heart to tell her that she's a bit late to the party. Plus, Theo threw a real zinger at her, so it's best to just keep things moving.

"I'm okay now. Thank you for stepping in when you did. When did you get here anyway?"

"I actually just walked in the door when I saw what was happening. A few friends and I decided to grab a drink." Ulgan points to the group of males beside him. "It looks like we came just in time. But it also looks like you had it handled all on your own. You seemed ready to deck him." He chuckles briefly, but concern is still written all over his face.

"Damn straight I would have. Nobody puts their hands on me without an invite." My fists clench again, the anger still simmering within me.

Fuck every single man who feels that they are owed a woman's time. Women should be able to exist and have fun without having to worry that some creep is going to touch them or force their company on them.

"An invite, huh? How does one go about securing an invitation?" He's completely taken my mind off of the asshole, and made me laugh. I'm so thankful he's here.

"If you play your cards right, you just might find yourself with one soon." His eyebrows shoot up with surprise, and he lets out a roar of laughter. "Why don't you and your friends come and join mine? We have plenty of room." I point toward our booth in the corner. In all honesty, I'm a bit shaken up and his presence makes me feel safe.

"Sounds good to me," Theo replies, gathering two other men and following Ulgan and I over to the booth. Rue, Hannah, and Isla aren't far behind.

We all stuff ourselves into the booth.

Ulgan and Theo introduce themselves to Hannah and Isla, and then we all get to meet their friend Declan, a charming troll who owns a construction company.

I'm so glad we ran into the guys. Ulgan has his arm wrapped protectively around my shoulders, and I can't lie, his growly protective side earlier was sexy as hell. My panties are soaked right now.

Theo offers to go and grab another round of drinks for everyone. "Hey Ada, want to come with me?" he asks, gesturing toward the bar. I leave the booth and walk over with him to wait at the bar for our next round.

Theo isn't at all what I expected. He always seems so put together and stoic, so to find out that he's funny as hell is a pleasant surprise. Obviously, he has to be a good guy if Ulgan calls him his best friend, but I didn't realize how charming he is.

Theo and Rue have had this weird tension between them for years, so I wasn't sure what would happen when I met him. She made him sound like a pompous ass, but he couldn't be farther from it. It didn't escape my attention, however, that he enjoyed getting Rue riled up. Seeing the exchange in person, I think my dear best friend enjoyed it a little more than she led on. Their weird tension seems more like sexual tension. I know they grew up together in Whispering Springs, but there must be more to their backstory than I know. Guess I'll just have to sit back and see how this plays out.

"Ada, I hope this doesn't sound awkward, but I feel like I already know you. Don't tell Ulgan this, but he talks about you all the time. I think he might be smitten," Theo says, leaning up against the bar.

He talks about me? I probably should be embarrassed for how happy this makes me, but I can't seem to give a damn.

"You think so, huh?"

"I know so." The sincerity in his voice is evident.

Now I have some questions for this handsome elf.

"If I asked you something, would you be honest with me?"

"Of course. Ask away." Theo replies with a kind smile.

"Is Ulgan really as wonderful as he seems? Obviously, you're his best friend, but it's hard for me to believe that someone like him exists."

"I've known the jolly green giant for most of my life. We've been friends since we were kids, and I can tell you without any hesitation that he is the best man I've ever met," Theo says. "What you see is what you get with him. Ulgan has always felt like he needed to prove himself, to prove his worth to those around him. Sometimes, he doesn't recognize just how much of a great guy he is. Any woman *or* purple-haired human would be blessed by the Goddess to get to be on the receiving end of his goodness and love."

My heart feels like it's going to burst with relief and joy. He really is as amazing as he appears.

"I can sense that you might have another question for me. Don't be shy, I'll sit here all night hyping him up. Hit me with it." He gestures with his hands for me to bring it.

My voice gets lower, almost to a whisper, as I say, "I've been burned so many times." I stop, unable to get my actual question out.

Theo puts his arm around my shoulder and pulls me close. His voice is filled with compassion. "He won't hurt you. I don't think he would even be capable of hurting you without it devastating him. It's safe to let him in."

In one fell swoop, Theo addressed the ugly fires of doubt and fear burning within me and doused them with water, smoldering the blaze.

Ulgan is fortunate to have a friend like Theo. One day, I would like to be able to count Theo as one of my friends as well. Everyone should have someone like him in their life.

Leaning into him, I whisper a thank you and his arm is lifted off of my shoulders. "We better return you to the table before the Incredible Hulk storms over here thinking I'm trying to put the moves on his girl." We laugh and bring the drinks back to the table.

Sitting next to Ulgan there is a noticeable shift in his mood. The moment I sit down he puts his arm around my shoulder and pulls me to his side with a low growl. Is he really jealous of Theo?

Let's fix that right now.

"You're lucky to have a friend like Theo. He was telling me how great you are." I take his hand from where it sits on his lap and hold it in mine. His body visibly relaxes, the tension melting off him.

"Plus, I've discovered I have a thing for men with tusks and tattoos."

He moves his larger body closer to mine, and my own grows hotter, wishing that we were alone so I could finally see what those big hands would feel like on my curves. The heat in his eyes is unmistakable.

"I think I know someone who fits that description, and he'd be happy to show you more than just his tusks any time you want," Ulgan says, inching closer to me with his gaze falling on my lips.

"Does anyone else feel like these two forgot they're at a table full of people who can hear them?"

Dammit, Rue. Well, I want to crawl under the damn table now. My hands come up to cover my face, as the table erupts into laughter. I peek through my fingers and see Ulgan shrinking in his seat, looking just as mortified.

"Leave them alone, guys," Hannah interjects. "They can't help it that they're so effing cute together."

Declan, Hannah's new admirer, pipes in, "Yeah, leave the lad and lass alone."

Hannah leans over and plants a kiss on his cheek, and the troll's green skin turns an even darker shade. Awe, someone's got a big old crush on Hannah.

An hour later, we pay our bills and each head home in separate directions, Isla having to leave first to pick up Kaida. I go over to the bar to thank Sebastian again for his help, but he is nowhere to be found. How interesting.

Rue decides to spend the night at my place, not wanting to go back to her own home. Ulgan drives us back in his Jeep since he didn't drink. He barely stops the car before Rue races out of the back seat and lets herself into my cottage to give us some privacy.

Ulgan hops out of the driver's side and quickly makes his way to my side of the car. He opens the passenger side door and holds his hand out to help me down. I probably should let go of his hand, but I just don't want to, so I keep hold of it as he walks me to my front door. Ulgan certainly doesn't appear to mind, a happy grin on his face.

"Thank you again for stepping in tonight. Your friends are so much fun."

"I'm glad you had a good time. They're really great guys. You don't need to thank me though, I'm just glad I could help." We stare at each other, not wanting this moment to end.

Ulgan takes a step toward me, leans down, and presses his lips to mine. His hands gently go to my waist, while mine run through his hair at the nape of his neck. I'm lost in the kiss, wishing it wouldn't stop. I want to stay like this forever, being held in his arms under the sparkling night sky.

Ulgan is just as breathless as I am when we stop. His eyes slowly travel over my face, as if he's trying to memorize every single one of my features. "Goodnight, Ada." His voice is deep and filled with need.

I stand on my tiptoes and place a gentle peck on his lips. "Goodnight, Ulgan." I turn to open my front door as he turns to walk back down the path of my driveway.

He shouts to remind me to lock my door before he hops back into his Jeep and drives away. It's a new feeling to have someone take care of me and worry about my safety. I'm so used to taking care of myself.

Walking into the living room, I find Rue already fast asleep on the couch, mouth open as she loudly snores. It looks like *someone* had a bit too much to drink tonight. After grabbing a blanket from a nearby chair and draping it over her, I head to my room to get ready for bed.

This night certainly was interesting. Ulgan was a complete surprise, and as much as I hate to admit it, his need to protect me turned me on like you wouldn't believe. As tempting as it is to pull out my favorite vibrator to help with the ache between my thighs, there must be some unwritten girl code rule about getting off while your friend sleeps just on the other side of the door.

Guess I'm going to bed wet and achy.

ten
ulgan

The soft crunch of wood shavings beneath my boots is a familiar sound as I enter my workshop. Woodworking had become a passion of mine in high school, after it'd been recommended to me as a creative outlet by a teacher. Baking is another passion of mine, but there's something about creating something permanent out of wood that calls to me.

Theo and I built my workshop the summer after high school when we were both bored and needed a way to stay out of trouble. We made plenty of mistakes, but in the end, it was a thing of beauty and something to be proud of.

Cranking the old stereo all the way up, the familiar drum beats of Green Day fill the space as I get to work.

The next few hours fly by as I sand down an oak table and apply a thin coat of stain to bring out the natural beauty. My mother has been in need of a new table for quite some time, and this will look just right at her place.

"Hey, man!" Theo yells from the door to the workshop. He

crosses the room and turns down the music. "I figured I'd find you here. The table's really coming along."

"The sanding was a pain in the ass, but it thankfully decided to cooperate."

"So, want to talk about last night?"

"What about?" The part where I almost ripped a fucker's face off for touching what's mine, or the part where my dumb ass actually got jealous of my best friend for talking to my mate? There is so much to choose from.

"Don't play dumb with me. I've known you for years and you've never so much as raised a hand to anyone, but last night you were ready to beat the shit out of that guy." Theo's voice is laced with concern. "Are you okay?"

"It's definitely not my proudest moment, but the way he was disrespecting her and grabbing her made me see red. Maybe it has something to do with the suppressants I've been taking, because I've never been so close to snapping before."

"The suppressants to prevent your mating heat? Are you even supposed to be on them so long? It's probably been months since you started taking them. Could they be starting to not be effective anymore?" The look of worry on Theo's face isn't a shock. Suppressants are supposed to be a temporary fix, not a permanent solution.

I've been on the mating heat suppressants since Ada walked into my life. When an orc scents his mate for the first time, it triggers an intense arousal which only goes away when we claim our mates. There is no way I'm going to act like a horn dog around Ada before she's ready, so the suppressants make it possible to be around her without whipping my cock out.

"I'll take them for as long as I need to until she feels safe with me. A little discomfort now will be worth it."

"Not for nothing, but that guy totally deserved what happened to him, or should I say 'allegedly' happened to him. No one should force themselves on anyone or use the words he did toward her."

I can't help but give a light chuckle as Theo gets himself worked up about what happened to my mate. He's a good guy, and I'm glad my friend feels protective of her already.

"I had a great time getting to know Ada last night, by the way. She's got it bad for you, man. You are one lucky son of a bitch to be fated to a woman like her."

"Yeah, sorry about glaring at you. I know you weren't making a pass at her, but after seeing that asshole touch her it made my not-so-subtle primal side flare up."

"No worries, I could have taken you." The cocky shit leans against the wall of my shop with his feet and arms crossed looking like he doesn't have a care in the world.

"In your dreams. Without the elf magic you've got, you wouldn't stand a chance."

"Sure, you keep thinking that. I'll lull you into a false sense of security and then BAM—you won't know what hit you." He balls up his fist and slams it into his other open palm dramatically.

Keep dreaming, elf.

"Seriously though, I'm here if you ever need to talk about this. Just be careful with those suppressants, okay?" The concern is back in Theo's voice.

"Thanks for looking out for me, man. I really appreciate it." I pull him in for a quick hug.

Theo leaves shortly after and I'm able to get back to working on the table a bit more.

My phone rings just as I'm about to head back to the apartment to get cleaned up. Rowley, one of the leaders of the pixies that live in Whispering Springs, needs some help putting up his tent for the fall festival. Of course, I'm happy to help, and let him know that I'll be there in a few minutes after a quick shower.

It's always been difficult for me to feel like I belong. Helping others around town with small projects makes me feel needed and wanted. It's a part of me that I've been working on in therapy, the part of me that needs to feel wanted by others even if it means overextending myself.

Heading inside to get cleaned up, my mind wanders back to Ada. After stripping off my sweat soaked jeans and shirt, I hop into the shower and allow the warm water to soothe my tired muscles.

Images of my Sunshine in the shower with me bombard my brain. Closing my eyes, I can picture her glorious body, all softness and curves, naked in front of me. My hand wanders down to my now angry cock and I begin to pump back and forth, wishing it was her hand. Loud moans echo around the bathroom as I continue to touch myself, imagining her mouth on me, sucking me deep down her throat. Her hands working my length while those beautiful blue eyes of hers watch me.

I'm close now, and I pump harder. Dream Ada would wrap her legs around my waist, holding onto my shoulders for dear life as I guide my dick into her sweet body. Goddess, I bet her pussy is tight and would feel amazing around my cock.

Suddenly, I'm pulled back to reality as my body explodes and cum shoots onto the shower wall. I have to brace my hand on the wall to keep upright since my legs decide they no longer need to hold me up. My breath is ragged as I come down from my orgasm.

Fuck, I need the real thing. This fantasy was good, but making love to Ada and showing her how much I care for her would be perfection.

I quickly finish up my shower and get dressed so I can help Rowley. My shower took much longer than expected, but damn did it feel good. After making sure my apartment is locked up and Benji is all set at the bakery, I head over to the town square.

eleven
ada

The Blackwood family has resided in the area where Whispering Springs was established centuries before humans decided that it would be the perfect place to settle. The walk up to Blackwood Estate is something that has to be seen to be believed. The long driveway is flanked up and down on both sides by massive weeping willow trees that sway gracefully in the wind.

Blackwood Estate sits on over a hundred acres, with each family in the coven receiving a parcel of the land so that they can build their homes. The entire property has been protected by powerful wards for generations, providing the coven a sense of safety against rival covens.

Rue's coven, The Blackwoods, have historically never had a great relationship with their neighboring coven, The Hawthornes. Angeline cannot stand their leader, Gareth Hawthorne. I believe if memory serves me correctly, she refers to him as "a dishonorable egomaniac with a questionable fashion sense."

Those two have a real Montagues and Capulets thing going on between them. Rue has always been puzzled over the real reason why they hate each other, but Angeline never gives a straight answer. She always gives a cryptic response about Gareth and his people using forbidden magic, but never goes further. Whatever the reason, I trust Angeline's judgment and steer clear of him on the rare occasions that he ventures into town.

The main house where Rue and her mother live is a three level Victorian that looks straight out of a Halloween movie. The dark exterior with black iron accents give it a sinister vibe that couldn't be farther from the truth. Outside of being the ideal location for a badass haunted house, it is also the source of so many of my happy memories. I remember the summers that Rue and I spent helping her mother in the community garden where they grew herbs and plants for spells and remedies. We even had our own *Practical Magic* inspired midnight margaritas one night after watching the movie.

Rue's black cat and alleged familiar, Hecate, is curled up on the front porch when I arrive. Reaching down and giving her a scratch behind the ears, her low satisfied purr let me know that she appreciates it.

"Hecate, is Rue home?" The cat cocks her head toward me, giving me a thoughtful look with her gleaming yellow eyes. I shit you not, the fluff ball points her head toward the front door and meows.

Maybe Rue wasn't lying when she said that Hecate wasn't just a regular house cat.

"Thanks, girl." Giving her a light kiss on the top of her head, I enter the house.

The inside of the house, if you can even call this mansion a house, is filled with luxurious antique furniture, large paintings depicting the gods and goddesses that the coven has worked with, and the most painfully beautiful stained glass windows.

"Rue, are you here?"

"Ada, is that you, honey?" Angeline Blackwood appears from one of the rooms off the sitting room. She's become a mother figure for me since Rue brought me home like a stray to spend the holidays with them.

"Hi, Angeline. Have you seen Rue?"

"I think she's up in her room. Why don't you check upstairs. It's good to see you, Ada. Are you free to stay for lunch today?"

"Of course. You know I never turn down any of your cooking. See you later." I give her a quick wave before walking up the side of the grand staircase that's straight out of a fairytale. It would be perfect for making a grand entrance.

At the top of the steps, I hang a right and find myself outside of Rue's bedroom. The door is open and her voice sounds from inside.

"Where the hell did I put those stupid earrings?" Her head is buried in a large box of jewelry.

"Everything okay over there?" I kick off my shoes and take a seat on her unmade bed.

Rue's never been one for keeping her room tidy. In fact, it always looks like a category four hurricane has just torn through it. Her closet has exploded all across the room, with vintage band tees, leggings, bras, and kimonos in every pattern you could imagine taking up residence on her floor. Open spell books are scattered across her desk, with vials of who knows what surrounding them.

"This pair of black moonstone earrings went missing," she whines and continues digging. With a grunt, she gives up. "Give me a second."

Rue closes her eyes and a soft glow of white light emanates from her hands. Appearing in her upturned palms are the earrings.

“That's more like it,” she says with satisfaction, putting the earrings on as she comes over to sit with me on the bed.

“Thanks for coming over today. Preparations for Samhain are doing my head in, and since you love me so much, I know that you’ll be willing to help me,” Rue says sweetly, batting her eyelashes.

I laugh and shake my head. “You know how much I love Samhain, so of course I’m in. What do you need help with?” Samhain, also known as the Witches New Year, marks the midpoint of autumn. It’s a magical time of year.

“Will you help me collect some things from the garden that we’ll need for the offerings and intention candles?”

“Can I pretend that I’m in a Victorian era period drama, walking through the garden while waiting for my husband to come back from war?” I ask, trying not to laugh.

“Of course you can. It wouldn’t be a trip to the garden if you didn’t,” she says seriously, but I can tell from the way her lip is twitching that she’s trying to not smirk.

“Okay, I’m in. Lead the way, my witchy friend.” I grin at her before we leave the room and head downstairs. We link arms, grabbing baskets on our way out into the garden. This will be the final harvest of the season so there’s a lot of work to be done.

Two hours later, we are sweaty and covered with dirt. Our baskets overflow with calendula, chrysanthemum, sage, marigolds, and even acorns that we found from around the property. We head back to the main house to drop off our baskets, clean up and relax.

Shouts ring out from inside of the house as we get closer to the door. We run in and are met with mayhem.

"Hecate, you demon cat! Put down my chicken!" Angeline chases after Hecate, who has a large rotisserie chicken in her mouth as she makes a run for it.

"Rue, your daughter is a complete menace," Angeline says. "She jumped onto the counter when I wasn't looking and stole the chicken that was meant for lunch."

"Don't call her a menace. She's a sweet little angel. Hecate, put the chicken down and walk away."

I'm not quite sure why Rue thought that would work, but Hecate looks Rue up and down before making off with the chicken.

"Oh, you little furry bitch!" Rue turns to Angeline. "Sorry, Mom. I'll give her a serious talking to tonight. How about the three of us pop into town for lunch, my treat?"

"Just so we're clear, I'm ordering a burger, fries, and a shake. That little demon cat made me need chocolate." We all laugh as Angeline grabs her bag and we head into town for lunch.

After lunch, Angeline heads home while Rue and I go to The Enchantress to pick up some items needed for the celebration. On our way to the shop, we walk down Main Street where business owners and vendors are setting up for the Fall Festival this coming weekend.

"Ada!"

I would recognize that voice anywhere. Turning around, I spot Ulgan helping a group of pixies set up their tent. With one final upward push, the tent is up, and I get to see that boy's rippling muscles in action.

He walks over to us with a big smile on his handsome face. "Hi ladies, it's good to see you both. Had a busy day?"

"We've just been at Rue's house prepping for Samhain. Are you helping set up for the festival?" I ask, trying to play it cool and not act like a high schooler with a crush.

"I just stopped over for a few minutes to help with the tent. It was giving them a little trouble," he explains.

Rue grabs my arm. "Hey, I'm going to head to the shop. Meet me there when you're done." She turns to Ulgan. "As always, it's a pleasure to see you and those glorious muscles of yours," she says before she disappears up the street.

I can't help but roll my eyes and laugh. "Please ignore her. She forgets how to behave in public. Are you looking forward to the festival?"

"Actually, I'm glad that I ran into you. I was wondering, if you aren't already busy, if you'd like to go with me. As my date. To the festival." He nervously adjusts his glasses, awaiting my response.

His awkwardness makes him that much more adorable to me.

My heart races with nervous excitement. "I would love to go with you. Pick me up at my place?"

His grin grows by the second. "Yes! I'll absolutely pick you up." We continue to stare at each other for a moment too long before his eyes flick behind me. "Oh crap, there's a line outside of the bakery. I better get over there, but I'll see you tomorrow."

Ulgan has thankfully already started to walk away before I realize that I'm doing a happy dance in the middle of the town square. An older couple walking by me tries to stifle their giggles, but let them laugh. Nothing is going to stop my happiness or my killer dance moves right now.

I head over to The Enchantress and help Rue for a bit before heading home. Just as I enter my cottage, my phone lets me know that I have a text from Ulgan.

ULGAN

I'm excited to spend tomorrow with you, Sunshine. I'll pick you up at your house around 9.

ADA

I can't wait! It was sweet of you to ask me. I'll warn you though, I am obsessed with this time of year so prepare yourself for me geeking out.

ULGAN

You're a fan of Halloween. I'll make sure to remember that. How do you feel about scary movies?

ADA

I freaking hate them, LOL. I'm a huge scaredy cat. However, I'd be open to watching one as long as you hold me when I'm scared...

ULGAN

DONE. I will do that for you anytime, Sunshine.

ADA

My hero! I'll see you tomorrow <3

ULGAN

Goodnight, Ada

THE NEXT MORNING, Ulgan picks me up and we walk over to Main

Street hand in hand to find that it's already overflowing with people.

"Since this is my first Fall Festival, what do you recommend we try?" I'm bubbling with excitement. Big community events like this just weren't done in my hometown, but I always saw them in movies and wished I could go.

"Well, in my expert opinion," he says, placing a hand over his heart, "I think that you need to experience Mable's locally famous spiced apple cider. But the way she tells it, it's world famous."

I love seeing this light hearted side of him, and that he's opening up more to me.

I let out a light sigh when he slings his arm across my shoulders and guides me over to a decorated stall that's been designed to look like a witch's cauldron, smoke wafting out and adding an eerie feel. It's only once we are at the stall that I recognize Mable. She's the slightly eccentric librarian at the town library and also a member of the coven. Hannah says that Mable may be a bit kooky, but she has the biggest heart around. She's dressed like a mad scientist, her white hair sticking up in every direction, giving her the appearance of someone that's jammed their finger in a light socket.

"Can I tempt you two beautiful specimens—I mean customers—to try some of my scrumptious spiced cider?" she says, while lights flash overhead and she pretends to experiment on a human brain made of jello. Well, I sure hope it's just jello.

"Hi Mabel, how's the festival going for you? Have many customers?" Ulgan greets her.

"Oh it's been wonderful so far. This might be the biggest turnout we've had in over a decade."

"That's awesome to hear! Ada, what would you like?" Ulgan

gestures toward a hopefully pretend hanging skeleton holding a menu.

"I've heard so much about this famous spiced cider, so I'd love a cup," I answer with maybe a bit too much excitement. I'm a sucker for fall flavors, and what's more fall than spiced cider?

"Make that two, please," he says to Mabel, pulling out money and handing it to her. "My treat." he says to me with a wink. I give his arm a playful squeeze.

"Thank you." I smile at him.

We get our ciders and stroll along the elaborate displays. Enchanted skeletons dance outside of one stall as a group of children laugh and dance along with them. Pumpkins of every color and size line the streets with candles flickering inside. The front of the library has been turned into a spooky graveyard complete with eerie fog, ancient looking tombstones, and enchanted ghosts swooping between people. This really is a fantastic event. I've run into students multiple times today, and each time Ulgan waits patiently, usually with a grin, so that I can say hello to them.

"Your students and their families really love you. I feel like I'm walking around with a celebrity," Ulgan says, sounding both proud and impressed.

"Thank you for being so wonderful and not getting upset that we kept getting stopped," I reply, feeling a bit awkward.

"Why would I get upset? I still remember how cool it was to run into my teachers outside of school. You're making an impact on them, and it goes to show how wonderful you are that they wanted to make sure that they could talk to you today," Ulgan says, giving me a gentle smile.

Could this man be any more perfect?

"A few guys that I've dated in the past wouldn't have been so patient. They probably would've stormed off, so I really appreciate it."

Ulgan's entire demeanor shifts. We were having a good time, and now his body is tense and he looks upset.

We continue to walk in silence for a minute before I hold his arm to stop him from walking further. "Ulgan, did I say something wrong? I thought we were enjoying ourselves, but you seem angry about something."

His eyes soften toward me and he lets out a breath it appears he had been holding. "I'm sorry, Sunshine. You could never do anything wrong, and I apologize that I made you feel that. You mentioning how human males have mistreated you in the past made me want to hunt each of them down and make them regret ever being unkind to you. No one should have to walk on eggshells around a partner, least of all you. You deserve to be cherished and taken care of, not asked to dim your light to make some guy's already dull light shine brighter." The anger appears to leave his body, and he looks at me like I'm something precious and worth fighting for.

I've never felt that from a man before.

It's hard to describe just how much his words mean to me, so I crook my finger, signaling him to bend down. He gives me a curious look but obeys. Once he's close enough, I kiss his lips, trying to convey all of the emotions swirling around inside of me.

The kiss ends far too quickly, but this is just one in a series of thousands I plan to give him. A laugh bursts out of me as he peers down with fogged up glasses.

"Wow, that was one hot kiss," he says, wiping his glasses off.

"Nice dad joke," I snort and immediately cover my mouth, horrified that it escaped.

"None of that. Don't hide from me." He grabs my hand. "That

was adorable." We continue walking through the maze of people and activities.

Ulgan stops to chat with various people from the town, introducing me to anyone I haven't yet met. Everyone is unbelievably kind and makes me feel at ease. It's hard to believe that a place like this exists.

A tent has been erected in the town square for pumpkin carving. I grab Ulgan's hand and drag him over to the massive tent as quickly as I can.

The woman at the table near the entrance smiles at us. "Are you two here to carve a pumpkin?" she asks.

I look up at Ulgan who nods and says, "I've never carved one before, but I think I can manage."

My jaw drops to the floor. How has he never carved a pumpkin? This needs to be rectified immediately.

"Oh, we are absolutely carving a pumpkin now!" I tell Ulgan. He takes the oversized pumpkin from the woman, and we find a spot at one of the many long rectangular tables under the tent.

We quickly come up with a design, a friendly but slightly confused looking jack o'lantern, and then Ulgan gets to work carving the top off. When it's time to remove the guts, the look of horror on his face definitely makes getting up early on the weekend worth it.

"People really do this for fun?" he asks, holding up a handful of stringy orange pumpkin guts.

"My granny and I would carve pumpkins for Halloween every year together, and save the seeds to roast for a snack later," I share. My heart aches, wishing that we could do that just one more time.

"Where did you go there for a second?" he asks thoughtfully.

"I was just thinking that she would have loved all of this, and how much I miss her," I say, holding out my arms and gesturing to everything around us.

"Why don't you tell me about her while I finish scooping out this crap," he chuckles, placing more of the pumpkin guts into the bowl between us.

We work side by side on our pumpkin creation as I share my favorite memories of Granny. How fearless she was, and how she loved with her entire heart. "She was a force to be reckoned with," I tell him with pride.

"You must take after her then," Ulgan says, tucking a stray piece of hair behind my ear. "Oh no, don't move. I got some pumpkin in your hair." We laugh as he tries his best to get rid of the pumpkin goop with a paper towel. It's been so long since I laughed this much.

We both take a step back to admire our slightly confused, but still adorable-looking pumpkin. The woman at the counter hands Ulgan a small tea light for us to put inside, and we make our way over to the display of pumpkins that others have created. He places our pumpkin among the others, and I notice something written in black ink on the side.

It reads: **U+A**, with a small heart around it.

Oh my gosh! He must've snuck that on there when I wasn't looking.

He reaches for my hand and we resume strolling through the festival. We come across Isla and her adorable daughter Kaida. The six year old is bouncing with excitement, wanting to go everywhere at once.

"Auntie Ada!" Kaida partially shifts, her cute dragon wings fluttering behind her, as she flies right into my open arms.

In just a few short months, this little cutie has me wrapped around her even cuter little finger. She asked me after that first day that we met if she could call me Auntie, and it touched me so deeply. I hope that any kids I have in the future are just as spunky as she is.

"There's my little peanut! Are you having a good time, sweetie?" I say, peppering her cheeks with kisses, making her squeal with glee.

"Mama and I carved punkins." Oh my heart. *Punkins.*

"Oh, you did? I bet it was the most beautiful pumpkin carved today. Ulgan and I carved a pumpkin, too," I tell her, pointing in his direction.

Without hesitation, Kaida flies out of my arms and right into his. The look on his face is priceless, not expecting her to fling herself at him. He catches her with an *omphf* and we all laugh at her fearlessness. This girl has never met a stranger.

"Are you Auntie's boyfriend?"

That little shit.

Without hesitating, he answers, "I'm unfortunately not, but I'd really like to be."

My mouth drops open, stunned. An odd feeling washes over me. A weird mix of excitement and hesitation.

"Auntie Ada, do you like him? I like him, and you should too. He has horns. Mama, can I have horns?"

"They're actually called tusks. You can touch them if you want," he says patiently. She reaches out and pokes one of his tusks with her index finger.

"Mama, do dragons grow tusks?"

Isla chuckles. "No sweetie, unfortunately for you, we don't. Sorry Ulgan, she just gets excited when she meets new people." Isla's eyes wander to something or someone behind Ulgan, and her demeanor changes. She seems distracted and a bit flustered.

She pulls me aside. "Can you watch Kaida for a little bit? I need to handle something and don't want to bring her with me." Her words are rushed. Was that Sebastian standing over there?

"Of course I can. Is everything okay?"

"Thank you, Ada. I'm fine, just need to take care of a problem." She turns back to Kaida. "Sweetie, you're going to hang out with Ada for a little while. I'll come and find you in a bit, okay?"

"Yay! Can I get my face painted, Auntie?" she asks, giving me her best puppy dog pout.

"Of course, peanut. We'll meet you over there, Isla," I say, shooing her away.

Ulgan places Kaida on his shoulders, and we walk over to the busy face painting tent. Kids choose designs from the illustrations on the walls before heading over to one of the high school art students that are volunteering.

We walk along the walls so that Kaida can pick out what she wants, and after changing her mind multiple times, she settles on a bright unicorn. She, of course, has the young girl painting her face add plenty of glitter when it is finished. Admiring her unicorn in the small hand held mirror, she whirls around to Ulgan.

"You should get a unicorn, too! We can be unicorn twins!" She's practically bursting with excitement at the prospect.

"Peanut, I don't think—" I start.

"I would be honored to be unicorn twins with you." He turns to the girl doing the face painting. "Only if you have time."

"Of course!" She grins. "Take a seat."

Ulgan's going to make an incredible father one day. My panties are melting watching him interact with Kaida. Am I weird for being completely turned on right now?

Almost as if he's a mind reader, his eyes lock on mine and his nostrils flare. He gives me a knowing smirk and returns his attention to Kaida, who can't get enough of him.

"Make sure to add extra glitter. He needs to sparkle just like me," Kaida requests.

"Um, there was a word missing in that request, little missy," I say.

"Sorry! Can you *please* add extra glitter?" The painter gives her a thumbs up and really goes to town with the glitter.

Ulgan rivals a disco ball, and I couldn't be more here for it.

"Holy shit." Isla appears next to me, covering her smirk with her hand. She definitely saw Ulgan. "Girl, you need to snatch up that man ASAP. He's a freaking keeper."

She addresses Ulgan now, "Ulgan, you have never looked better."

Kaida flies over to Isla, excited to show off her little unicorn.

"Mama, look what Ulgan and I did! He's my unicorn twin!" Kaida proudly shows off her face paint.

"Oh, I see that baby. You both look sparkly and fabulous." Isla gives her daughter a hug. "Thank you both so much for watching her. Okay, Kaida, we have to head home to see grandma. She is going to love your face paint. Can you say thank you to Ada and Ulgan?"

Kaida waves to us, snuggling into her mom's side. "Bye Auntie Ada! Bye Ulgan! I hope she lets you be her boyfriend!"

The two leave us, and I can't help but give him a hug.

His muscular arms wrap around me, and I sneak a peek at them. They're just so delicious. He chuckles and says, "What's this for? Not that I'm complaining. You can touch me whenever you want."

"You just keep surprising me. You were amazing with Kaida," I answer, speaking into his chest.

"She's adorable, and clearly loves you very much," he says.

I pull back to look at him, but he still holds me close. "Were you serious when you said that you wanted to be with me?" My voice shakes. I hate feeling vulnerable like this.

Please don't let this be some cruel joke.

"I've never been more serious in my life. Getting to know you has made me happier than I've ever been. I'm in awe of you, and just want to be with you all the time." he says, looking at me with such tenderness.

"So, does this mean we're together?" I ask, needing a definitive answer.

"Yes, Sunshine. You're stuck with me."

That weird feeling still sits heavy in my chest, but I decide to bury it and allow myself to be happy.

I deserve to be happy.

Hours later, we're outside my cottage after he walked me home, and I'm wishing the day didn't have to be over.

"What are you doing tomorrow?" I ask him. "I have the day off and thought it might be fun to go see that new superhero movie."

"I would love to, but I can't tomorrow. I already have a date," he replies casually.

Is he dating someone else? Didn't we *just* say we were together now? Embarrassment and insecurity rears its ugly head, and I just want to run into the house. I should've known this was too good to be true.

"Okay, well, have fun I guess," I say, trying to keep my voice steady as I turn to go hide inside. Ulgan must notice the shift in my mood, because his hand wraps around my wrist to stop me as I start to go back in the house.

"Ada, it isn't that kind of date," he says, words tumbling out of his mouth.

"Isn't there only one kind?" I fail at hiding how hurt my feelings are. "I'm not the type of woman who'd be okay being in a relationship with someone who's seeing other people."

Ulgan pulls me close to him so that there is little space between us, and I can feel his heart pounding in his chest. "No. Please let me explain. When I was growing up there was this kind neighbor who would watch my sister and I so our mom could work. She's gotten older and lives at a nursing facility now. She and I have a 'date' once a month to catch up. I'm seeing her tomorrow," Ulgan says breathlessly.

Oh, well now I feel like an asshole for being upset. It's so ingrained in me to compare him to the men from my past, but I'm working on it.

"Oh, that's really sweet," I say. "It's wonderful that you go to visit her. We can go to a movie some other time. She's lucky to have someone thoughtful like you to care."

"I had a lot of fun today," Ulgan says. "I'll talk to you soon?"

"Text me so I know you got home safe. Have a good night."

I turn to grab the front door knob when his hand covers mine. I give him a questioning look over my shoulder.

"Would you want to come with me? Obviously, you don't know Miss Laurel, but it'd be nice to have some company." Ulgan shifts from side to side, looking unsure of himself. "You know what, you probably wouldn't want to come. You'd be stuck with me in the car for an hour and—"

"I'd love to go with you," I blurt, interrupting him.

"Really? Are you sure? I don't want you to feel pressured to come," he says, nervously adjusting his glasses.

"I don't do anything I don't want to do. I'd love to keep you company." I pull him toward me and put my arms around his shoulders. "Are you positive she won't be uncomfortable with a stranger coming? I know she means a lot to you."

"She's going to love you. How about I pick you up tomorrow at nine?" His hands settle on my waist.

A sudden wave of shy excitement washes over me. "Sounds great. Will there be coffee involved?"

"For you? Always." Ulgan winks at me before leaning over to give me a short sweet kiss.

Of course, it would've been sweet if I didn't pull him closer to kiss him deeper. I just can't help myself around him.

LATER THAT NIGHT, my mind starts to wander, and I imagine what a future would look like for Ulgan and me. The longer I live in Whispering Springs, the more I learn about all of the different types of monsters that are my neighbors. Each with their own unique histories, culture, and even anatomical differences.

Honestly, I don't know much about orcs beyond the basics. This needs to change right now, since Ulgan and I are officially together.

It's time to research the shit out of orcs.

Like any good researcher, I lay out a shit ton of snacks, grab every orc romance novel off of my bookshelves, and set up my laptop with a strong internet connection.

My source material is written by the greatest orc authors of our time. I flip through the pages of the novels scattered around me and take notes in my notebook, while balancing my laptop on my thigh for any quick online searches I may need to do to confirm my findings.

By the end of the night I'm sufficiently exhausted, but happy with the information I've learned. Hannah would be proud of my fact checking skills and the sheer amount of resources I combed through.

I stare at the notes that I've written, and a few questions arise. Of course, right now probably isn't the best time to ask Ulgan, since our relationship is brand new, but it certainly gives me some things to think about.

1. Orcs have fated mates that they bond with forever. It's an ancient biological pull toward their perfect life partner. Would humans feel this bond?

2. When orcs find their mate it triggers a mating frenzy. This sounds fun

3. Mating frenzy equals knotting and loads of sex. An orc's knot is at the base of their cock and swells inside of their mate to make sure that they get pregnant. This intrigues me...especially after that image search I did.

4. Orcs have a primal instinct to provide shelter for their mates. Someone wants to build me a house? I'm sold!

5. Orcs appear to be excellent in bed. This may just be because my source material is mainly romance novels, but I'm sold, again!

Closing my laptop, I leave my books stacked up on the coffee table, promising to myself that I'll put them away tomorrow. Putting on my softest pajamas, I climb into bed.

Even though exhaustion has hit me, I just can't seem to turn my brain off. Every time my eyes close, images of Ulgan swaggering toward me at the height of a mating frenzy flash in my mind. A big knot, ready to make me feel oh so good.

Is it getting hot in here?

I didn't even realize that my hand has slipped beneath my panties and is giving much needed attention to my clit. My breathless moans echo around the room as my fingers move through my slick core. I picture Ulgan in bed with me, with his strong hands working my body. I wish that it was him touching me between my thighs. Within moments, my back arches off of the bed and I'm experiencing a powerful and breathtaking orgasm. Ulgan's name screams from my lips.

My heart is racing and my body feels more relaxed. Pulling my fingers away, I fall into a peaceful sleep.

Tomorrow, I get to see the orc of my dreams.

twelve
ada

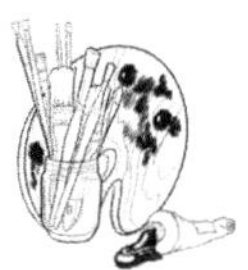

The next morning, Ulgan's forest green Jeep pulls up outside of my place. My palms are sweaty, and I find myself unable to sit still. Meeting Miss Laurel, someone that he cares deeply about, is important, and I don't want to mess this up.

By the time I make it to his Jeep, he's already by the passenger side door, holding it open for me. "You are looking awful pretty today, Sunshine," he says, eyes moving up and down my body.

"You know just how to make a girl feel special." I move closer to Ulgan until we are almost touching. Pulling on the collar of his jacket, he leans forward so that I can place a peck on his lips.

Hopping into the car, we leave behind Whispering Springs and start our hour-long drive to the city. He hands me my iced coffee and just the first sip instantly wakes me up.

The car ride is quiet as I go through every doomsday scenario in my head. What if I make a complete fool of myself and embarrass Ulgan so badly that he doesn't want anything to do with me anymore? Or, what if this whole thing between Ulgan and I is just in my head? Completely oblivious, it takes me a moment to realize that we've pulled over, and the car is stopped.

Did we pop a tire or something? Run out of gas, maybe? Those were not on my list of shit that could go wrong today, but now they are.

Ulgan turns in his seat to face me. "Ada, are you okay? I won't be upset if this is something that you don't want to do. We can turn around now and I can drop you off at home."

I not-so-gracefully throw my head back onto the head rest. "It's not that. I want to do this with you, and I'm honored that you asked me to come. I like you a lot, and just don't want to mess this up by acting weird in front of someone you care about."

"You're nervous that you'll act weird? Miss Laurel is a weird woman in her own right, so please don't worry about acting a certain way to impress her." Ulgan laughs to himself. "Her freak flag has been flying for decades, if not longer, so she's not one to judge anyone on anything. You are perfect just the way you are. Let her see the real Ada. She's pretty wonderful, but I'm biased since I like her a whole lot." He shoots me a reassuring smile.

"Let's put on some music and you can ask me anything you want about her," he says, handing over his phone. I start searching for a song that will put me in a good mood.

The car fills with a familiar tune that I always have to dance and sing along to. I even convince Ulgan to join my car dance party, and shockingly, the big guy has some moves. By the end of the song, I'm both breathless and my stomach hurts from laughing.

"Okay, what did you think?" I ask, knowing there is only one right answer.

"Well, I'm not sure how 'karma is a cat,' but the song was fun. Why don't you play another song that you like?" We listen to a few more of my favorites before I lower the volume. It's time to learn a bit more about Miss Laurel.

"Okay, buddy, it's time for a little Q&A. What kind of monster is Miss Laurel?" I ask, turning to face him while resting the side of my head against the seat. "Is she an orc like you?"

"No, actually Laurel is a dryad," Ulgan says. "I don't know if you've ever seen one before, but dryads are nature spirits that have a deep connection to trees. I'm anxious to see your reaction when you meet her, since you're an artist. Dryads are hauntingly beautiful. One thing that I should warn you about are her vines. They have a mind of their own, and tend to sneak up on you when you least expect it."

"She has vines? What do they do?" Now I'm more intrigued than nervous to meet her. I've never seen anyone with vines before.

"It's actually pretty interesting. I don't understand exactly how it works, but Laurel is able to sense someone's soul through the vines. They have to be touching someone to work. I've seen it a few times, and they've always been spot on."

"So, they can sense whether someone is a good person or not?"

"Kind of, but it's deeper than that. It's almost as if her vines can peer into a person's soul and uncover who they are at their core. I might not be explaining it correctly. It's one of those things that you need to see for yourself in order to understand."

We fall into a peaceful silence and I mull over what he's shared. I wonder what Miss Laurel's vines will sense if they touch me? I'm too curious to see them at this point to worry much.

"Is there anything that Laurel likes? Should we stop and pick something up for her?"

Ulgan glances at me with a smile. "That's actually a great

idea. She loves these doughnuts from a little shop near her nursing home. I've been trying to recreate them for her for years, but she always says that it's a good try, but not close enough." He chuckles. One of his hands leaves the steering wheel and rests on my thigh. His warmth seeps through the thin leggings I wore today. "Is this okay?" he says timidly.

I grab his hand and hold it in place, loving that he wants to touch me as much as I want to be touched. "Yeah, it's okay. Thank you for checking. I appreciate it."

He gives my thigh a gentle squeeze and focuses on the road. He couldn't possibly know how much it means for him to check in like that. It's one of the many reasons I feel comfortable with him. He always makes sure to go at my speed and not push me too far. I need to thank his mother for raising him right. You know, if I ever get the chance to meet her.

Live in the present, girl. Stop worrying about the future, and enjoy right now. My life is going really well, and I'm allowed to enjoy that instead of waiting for the other shoe to drop.

"Would it help your nerves if we keep talking?" he asks.

"That would be amazing." My whole body relaxes and I turn in my seat to face him.

"How about a game of 20 questions?" he suggests.

"Mr. Durzum, are you feeling nosy?" I tease.

Ulgan lets out a chuckle, and his cheeks darken.

"I'm in," I say. "You go first."

He clears his throat. "Okay, I'm going with some hard hitting questions first, so prepare yourself. You can only keep one: coffee or chocolate?"

"Easy, I'm picking chocolate. My turn: where's your happy place?" Mine is sitting in this car right now with him.

"It's going to sound boring, but probably my bakery. Baking brings me a sense of calm and happiness," he confesses.

"That's beautiful, Ulgan." I weave my fingers through his and rub his forearm. His kind eyes land on me before turning back to the road.

Ulgan shifts in his seat a bit before speaking again. "Describe your dream house."

Oh, he's really done it now. I've been dreaming about my future home since I was a little girl. My kind man sits patiently and listens as I describe each and every room of the house in painstaking detail.

I can see it now. The cape cod style house with a front porch where I could drink my coffee in the morning, the spacious bathtub for late night soaks, and of course, my own art studio. Ulgan sits for what feels like an hour listening to me ramble on. I normally would feel embarrassed for talking this much, but he makes me feel so comfortable. It also doesn't hurt that he seems completely invested in what I'm saying.

"You've really thought of everything. That sounds like a gorgeous home." He smiles at me.

My vision of my future begins to shift. I can now see Ulgan sitting on that front porch drinking coffee with me, soaking in that tub together, and supporting me in that art studio. A peaceful feeling settles in my chest as I allow myself a few moments to imagine this serene image. Just a few moments of bliss before reality sets in.

Not long after we pull up to the doughnut shop, make our purchases and finish our short drive to the facility. Ulgan holds my hand as we stroll down a winding hallway, stopping outside of room 13B.

His warm breath fans against my ear as he leans down and

whispers, "She's going to love you." His soft lips press against my cheek, the skin heating under his touch.

He knocks on the door, which swings open almost instantly, but no one is there. How...?

Peering into the suite, there is an intricately woven length of green vines covered in soft purple blooms that move through the room and back, as if they're being retracted. The vines stop at a small upholstered chair, weathered with time.

"Is that you Ulgan?" a melodic voice asks. "Because if it isn't, I may be old, but I'll still kick your ass."

Oh, she and I are going to get along just fine.

Ulgan shakes his head and lets out a hearty laugh. "Would you quit threatening people? Yes, it's me, and I brought someone with me that I want you to meet."

Miss Laurel lets out her own laugh. "Well, get yourself in here, then! Are those doughnuts I smell? Oh, you know the way to this old lady's heart."

I finally can see the small dryad. Her twisting vines resemble those of a wisteria tree, and she has a slightly humanoid face. Her skin is the color of rich antiqued wood, and her vibrant green eyes are piercing in contrast.

Setting the doughnuts on the coffee table, we sit on the sofa opposite her. I've never met a being quite like her before, her earthen beauty haunting.

"Now Ulgan, why don't you pretend like you have some manners and introduce me to your friend." Laurel's quick wit would put Rue to shame.

"Miss Laurel, this is my m—this is my girlfriend, Ada," he stumbles over his words. What on earth was he going to say?

"Girlfriend, huh? Is that what we're calling it these days? Anyway, Ada, it's so nice to meet you, love. How did you meet this big lug?" she asks, gesturing at Ulgan, who sits next to me with amusement clear on his face.

"We met at his bakery. He created a plan to get me to paint a mural there so he could spend time with me instead of just asking me out. Jokes on him, though. I had fun painting, and I already had a crush on him." I laugh and give him a playful nudge.

"*Oh*, I like you!" Miss Laurel exclaims. "I like you a whole hell of a lot." She wheezes, caught in a laughing fit.

Ulgan looks so smug right now. The hot bastard must've known that I wasn't visiting his bakery every morning because the coffee was that good.

We spend the next two hours eating way too many doughnuts and listening as Miss Laurel shares stories about Selene and Ulgan as kids. Apparently, he was a bit of a nudist.

"There he was, diaper off, naked as the day he was born, running up and down the street chasing a butterfly. It took me ages to catch him since the little bugger was so fast." Miss Laurel swipes tears from her eyes from laughing so hard.

"That must have been hilarious!" I clutch my stomach, laughing with my whole body.

"Oh, it was. He had the cutest little tush, but I'm sure you've already seen it so you know what I mean," Miss Laurel says, giving me an over dramatic wink. This lady has a dirty mind, and that makes me like her even more.

"And that's our cue to leave." Ulgan shoots up from the couch, looking embarrassed. "Miss Laurel, make sure to call me when you want to come visit Mom. I know she'd love to see you and catch up," he says, rubbing the back of his neck as his cheeks darken.

"I'm not shy, I'll be sure to call for my knight in shining green armor when I need him," Miss Laurel replies, giving him a hug. Ulgan walks over to the door, and Miss Laurel and I are now alone. She reaches for my hands and holds them in her own. "Ada, you simply must come back and visit me. Maybe we can even ditch this one and have a night out on the town."

"I would love that. Thank you so much for letting me crash your date today." I can't help the smile that's spread across my face. This has been such a great afternoon.

Miss Laurel pulls me in for my own hug, and before I even know what's happening, her vines have crept up my arms and wrapped me in their own embrace. A sharp intake of breath comes from me, my heart stopping as I hesitantly pull back to look at Laurel. A sense of calm washes over me as the vines almost pulsate against my skin.

Her face radiates pure happiness and joy. She pulls me back in for another fierce hug. "He's going to love you with his whole heart. Thank you for existing, sweet girl."

She brushes away the few tears that have escaped down my cheeks. It's then I realize she is crying as well. Miss Laurel and I walk arm in arm over to Ulgan who has been waiting patiently for me.

We leave her room and make our way back to the car. Walking with me over to the passenger side, muscular arms envelop me and I lean into Uglan's equally muscular chest.

"What did you think of her?" he asks, his lips moving against my hair.

"She's the best. I get why you visit her so often. I'll have to take her up on her offer of sharing more stories about you."

"She's certainly got plenty of them," he chuckles, planting a kiss on the top of my head before releasing me and opening up the passenger door. I slide inside, the Jeep dipping under his weight as he hops in, and we head back to town.

His hand reaches over the gear shift and takes up residence back on my thigh, his thumb rubbing slow circles.

His hand leaves my thigh for just a moment to hand me his phone. "Want to pick the music again?"

"How about you pick? What do you like to listen to?" Please, universe, don't let him like something like polka.

He pulls over for a second, taking the phone from me and selecting a song. "Remember, this is a judgment free zone, Sunshine."

Suddenly, 2000s emo music blasts through the speakers. This I can get behind. Who knew my man was into some of my favorite bands from when I was growing up?

"Do you mind if I turn this up? I freaking love this song!"

"Really? Hell yeah!" The volume is cranked and we're both singing at the top of our lungs, windows down.

This turned out to be the perfect day. The more I get to know about Ulgan, the harder I fall for him. Who am I kidding? I'm falling hard, and there's this nagging part of me that thinks this is moving way too fast. However, there is an even bigger part of me that can't get enough of him and knows that this feels right.

His hand is back on my thigh—where I've determined it belongs—and I thread my fingers through his. This feels right, and I need more of it.

thirteen
ada

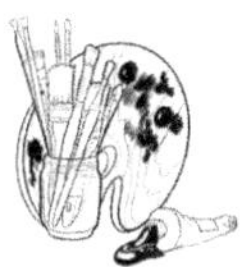

Wednesday evening, Ulgan calls me to see if I'm free to have dinner at his place on Friday. After accepting his invitation, I daydream about what that evening could bring. Will this be the time that we become more intimate? It's been awhile since I've had sex with anyone other than my dildo, Alfred.

Sharing my body with someone wasn't something that I'd enjoyed before, feeling self conscious of every little stretch mark or roll of my stomach. I'm in a much better place now with my body, thankfully, but I can't help but feel uneasy about being naked in front of someone new. Ulgan, has made it abundantly clear that he appreciates my body through his words and touch, but will he want to take the next step in our relationship?

There's no more time for me to worry, because just like that, it's Thursday and my students have their art night. It's a huge success, and it makes my heart soar to see each of my students proudly share their creations with their families. Then, before I know it, it's Friday night and my entire day at work has flown by.

Checking myself out in the mirror, I do a quick fluff of my

hair, loving how the big curls turned out. I keep my outfit simple with a sleeveless black dress and cute forest green cardigan. As a chronic overplanner, I made sure to wear my sexiest deep maroon bra and panty set, just in case he decides to have me for dessert. The set cost as much as my car payment, but Rue convinced me that I needed the almost sheer lingerie.

Applying my favorite perfume, I do a final once over and grab my bag before heading out the door. Ulgan lives in the apartment right above the bakery, and I get there in no time. A walkway behind the bakery leads to a staircase that stops just outside his front door. My heart flutters as I knock on the heavy wood.

The door opens, and Ulgan instantly pulls me into his arms. I giggle as he peppers my cheeks with little kisses. He pulls back and gives me one of his adorable grins. "You look incredible tonight," he says, looking over every inch of me slowly, heat in his eyes.

I move out of his grasp and give him a little twirl. "Oh, this old thing? You clean up pretty well yourself, Mr. Durzum."

Ulgan looks sexy as hell in a white button up shirt with the sleeves rolled up to put his muscular tattooed arms on display. His hair is out of its signature bun and hangs down to his shoulders. Ulgan does his own playful twirl so I can get an eyeful of him. The black jeans he's got on hug his ass just right, and I want nothing more than to grab it. The more I look, the more evident it is that my sweet orc is sporting a large bulge in the front of his pants.

"My eyes are up here, Sunshine," he says, his voice raspy and filled with need.

My cheeks are on fire, but honestly, I couldn't care less that I've been caught checking him out. Ulgan doesn't realize how much of a catch he is, so I've decided to show him just how badly I want him.

Getting closer to him, I place my hand on the back of his neck and pull him to me for a kiss. His arms wrap around me as we get lost in each other before pulling apart to catch our breath. "You are an amazing man, Ulgan. It also doesn't hurt that you're the sexiest man I've ever met."

He pulls away a bit and searches my face, as if looking to see if there was a lie anywhere in the comment. Suddenly, his eyes fill with happiness. It's impossible for me to hide how I feel about him. Is this moving quickly? Absolutely. Does this feel like it was meant to be? Definitely.

Is a small part of me panicking at how much I like him? The jury's still out on that one.

Suddenly, the apartment fills with a thick layer of smoke. "Oh shit, the lasagna!" he shouts, letting go of me and running to the kitchen. I have to place my hand over my mouth to stifle the laugh threatening to escape.

After a few stressful minutes, the formerly on-fire lasagna is now drenched in water and sitting in his sink. The two of us are in tears laughing as we open all of the windows to get rid of the smoke.

"Well, this night certainly didn't go as planned," he says, coming to sit next to me on his couch.

I finally got the chance to look around his apartment. It screams Ulgan. Cookbooks cover the shelves of what looks like a handmade bookcase. Huge oversized furniture to fit his larger size peppers the space, and framed photos of him, his family, and friends cover the walls. It's clear in the photos that he's loved very much by those around him, and it isn't hard to understand why.

One photo catches my attention in particular. It's an older

photograph, aged with time, of two small orc children, one boy and one girl. Both of them have similar lopsided toothy grins, and their joy is infectious. They hold up a fish between the two of them that they must've just caught.

This must be Ulgan and his sister. It had to have been fun to have a sibling to grow up with. I was always envious of classmates who had siblings when I was a kid. Siblings are like a built in best friend that you sometimes want to punch in the face.

"I'm sorry about dinner. Let me check the fridge to see what I can whip up." He goes to stand, and I grab his arm to stop him.

"How about you let me make dinner for you? My cooking skills aren't at your level, but I've been told that I make a mean grilled cheese."

He chuckles. "Grilled cheese is always a good time. How can I help?"

"How about you show me where you keep everything and then you can keep me company?"

"Yes, ma'am!" He salutes me, taking my hand and leading me to the kitchen. We work in companionable silence as I whip up the grilled cheeses. Every now and then I catch him staring at me with a goofy smile on his face. Does he notice how normal this feels? Us spending a quiet night in, chatting, and making dinner together?

We eat our grilled cheeses with a caprese salad that he'd already prepared. This guy already knows that cheese is the way to my heart.

After dinner, we move back to the couch where we watch a corny romcom. Throughout the movie we get closer to each other until he's stretched out on the couch with his head in my lap. He gives a satisfied moan as I massage his scalp and play with his soft dark hair, a stark contrast against my fair skin. His head nestled against my soft stomach brings me a sense of contentment. I can picture us, years from now doing this very thing.

He gently pulls my hand in front of his face and begins to place kisses to each of my fingers and my palm. I sigh, loving the attention. The movie forgotten, he carefully turns to look at me, cupping my face and pulling me down for a kiss. Our kiss starts out soft and lazy, but something shifts once I open my lips as an invitation for more. Ulgan doesn't hesitate as his tongue caresses mine, sipping from my mouth.

He pulls away briefly so he can sit up, and I quickly find myself straddling his legs. Those large hands grip my waist and pull me closer. The thick outline of his cock now presses just right against my core.

He looks to me for an okay before moving forward. I love a consent king, but I'm going to burst into flames if we don't do something. "Ulgan, touch me," I urge him, needing to feel his hands on me.

He tugs me down by the nape of my neck, lightly fisting his hand in my hair. We kiss passionately for what seems like hours, coming up for breath before picking right back up again. Ulgan kisses his way down my collarbone toward my sensitive breasts. I take off my cardigan and toss it on the floor behind me. His fingers grip the edge of my dress and pull it over my head before it joins the cardigan.

His eyes darken with desire as he takes in my lingerie. "Can you feel how hard you make me?" he asks, placing my hand against his cock, still trapped in his pants.

"You're wearing too many clothes, Ulgan." A whine leaves me. I need to see him, and I need to see him *now*.

My fingers make quick work of the buttons on his shirt, and he helps me pull his arms out of the sleeves. Flinging it over my shoulder, my attention is focused on the now deeply offensive pair of pants that stand between me and what I want. "Pants. Off. Now."

He throws his head back and roars with laughter. "You don't have to ask me twice."

Ulgan lifts me off of his lap and places me on the couch. He shucks off his pants and is now standing before me in the most sinful pair of black boxer briefs in existence. The outline of his cock has me almost passing out, its thickness alone making my pussy weep. I don't want to sound like a cliché from one of my romance novels, but holy fuck, how is that thing going to fit? Can you die from too large of a dick?

Death by dick *would* be a hilarious epitaph on my gravestone.

Pushing him back onto the couch, I take my rightful place straddling his lap. Even with the little amount of fabric still in the way, I grind my hips down on him, giving us the pressure that we both crave. His hands return to my hips, guiding them harder on him. Grinding against this man is so fucking hot, and no one can convince me otherwise. His tusks graze my breasts, leaving behind light red marks. As he places kisses along each curve, he releases a grunt of frustration that the bra is in the way. I slide my arms out of each strap and reach around behind my back to unclasp it. Finally, my breasts are free from their torture device. Ulgan's eyes intently look over my chest in appreciation.

"You're perfection," he moans under his breath. Collecting the bra from my hand, he tosses it to the ground.

In an instant his lips are wrapped around one of my dusky pink nipples, his wide tongue switching between circling the bud and lightly sucking. Our hips continue to grind together, the friction bringing me closer and closer to that delicious feeling that I'm chasing. He releases my nipple with a pop, and lavishes attention to the other.

A moan escapes me. "That feels so good."

Our hips frantically move, chasing release. "Oh, right there. Don't you dare stop," I demand.

"Never, love," he practically growls.

Within seconds I'm coming, shaking violently. A few more thrusts against my covered core and Ulgan is shouting my name. I collapse on top of him, trying to catch my breath. Our pants fill the apartment, both completely spent.

He cradles me to his body, and I can feel his heart beating rapidly. Nestled in the crook of his neck, I breathe in his masculine scent that's so uniquely him. This scent needs to be a candle or something.

"I need to taste you," he says. "Would you like that?"

My voice is apparently unable to work, all I can do is nod my head enthusiastically. He gets up with me still on his lap and we swap places. I lean against the back of the sofa while Ulgan positions himself on his knees in between my legs. Slowly, he works my panties down my legs until I'm bare before him.

Seeing him like this makes me ache all over again.

"Spread your legs wider for me, Sunshine. I need to see how wet that pretty pussy is for me."

Fuck, I'm going to spontaneously combust. Ulgan being a dirty talker was not on my bingo card.

"Look at you, love. You're positively soaking. Is this all for me?" He slowly runs his hands up and down my inner thighs, each time getting closer to where I really need him.

"Yes, it's all for you," my breathy reply leaves my lips. He hasn't even done anything and I'm already panting.

"You're such a good mate, getting all wet for me," he says,

his voice sounding gravelly and dripping with sexiness. "I wonder if you taste as heavenly as you smell? Should I find out?"

Did he just say *mate*?

Before I can reply or question it, his rough tongue flattens against my pussy and licks straight through. A cry bursts from me and I feel the rumble of his chuckle against my core.

"Mmm, you are so fucking delicious." He continues lapping at me, groaning with satisfaction with each swipe, his hands continuing to hold my thighs a part.

"Ulgan! Oh, your mouth feels incredible. Keep going!"

After several minutes of this exquisite torture, he hasn't paid attention to my clit, and I can't wait any longer.

"Baby, I need you to suck my clit. Please!" I have no issue asking for what I need.

Ulgan immediately begins to alternate between circling it and rougher flicks. I climb closer and closer to the edge, but when he finally pulls the flesh between his lips, I shatter.

One of the most intense orgasms I've ever had rips through me, and my entire body shakes as I shout his name in ecstasy. My thighs clamp down on either side of his head as he continues to slowly sip at my core, helping me through the orgasm and drinking down my cum.

Ulgan places light kisses on each of my inner thighs and raises himself up. His lower jaw is covered in my wetness, which he wipes off with the back of his hand. He slowly kisses his way up my body before capturing my lips in a passionate kiss. I can taste myself on him, and it's so damn hot.

Placing my hands on his chest, I softly push him away so that we are looking at each other. "Ulgan, that was freaking amazing."

He chuckles. "I'm glad you enjoyed that. I know I certainly

did." He leans down, kissing my neck and running his tongue over my pulse.

"Can I taste you?" I ask, rubbing my hand over his insanely still growing bulge.

"Ada, you don't have to," he says sweetly.

"Ulgan, I *need* to taste you," I whine, knowing that I *need* to have him in my mouth.

"Goddess help me, you're incredible," he says breathlessly. "Who am I to deny a beautiful woman what she wants?"

Swapping places with him on the couch, it's my turn to kneel before him. Leaning down, I place a kiss onto his cock through his underwear. He sucks in a sharp breath, cock twitching. Placing my fingers into the waistband of his briefs, I slowly wiggle them down as Ulgan raises his hips to help me finally get them off.

His thick cock bobs in front of my face. It's a lighter shade of green from the rest of him, with thick veins running down the entire length and ridges that look like a damn sex toy. His knot is on full display, a large swell at the base. A small amount of cum drips down the side, begging for me to lick it.

It takes me a second to get over how desperate I am to finally taste him. Slowly wrapping my fingers as far around his length as I can, I lower my lips to the leaking tip and begin lapping my tongue, collecting his precum. The taste of cinnamon hits my taste buds and I pull back. Does orc cum taste like cinnamon? Raising my head to ask Ulgan, I stop short when I see his head resting against the back of the couch, a look of pure bliss on his face.

My question can wait for later.

Going back to work, wrapping my mouth around him, my tongue massages the little ridges that run on either side of his cock. I know these are going to feel so freaking amazing inside of me. Ulgan's moans of satisfaction get louder the closer he gets to coming.

My hands work in tandem with my mouth, alternating between licking and sucking.

"You suck me so beautifully," he pants. "Your mouth is pure heaven. Be a good little mate and keep sucking me."

There it was again, him calling me *mate*. Was it just an accident in the heat of the moment?

I don't have any more time to think about it. His breath quickens. He gently fists my hair, and cums. I try to drink down as much as I can, but some escapes my mouth and runs down my chin.

Licking up the last of his cum off of his cock, I release him with a pop. I collect the cum from my chin with my index finger and playfully lick it off while locking eyes with Ulgan. I could get used to this whole flavored cum thing.

Ulgan places his hands under my arms and pulls me to lay on top of him on the couch. Rubbing my back in comforting circles he says, "Remind me to ruin dinner more often, if this is how the night will end."

I chuckle, snuggling in closer. "That was incredible." I hesitate. "Did you call me 'mate' while we were...?"

"Um, yeah I guess I did." Ulgan moves me off his lap and stands from the couch. "Ada, I need to talk to you about something." He begins nervously pacing the living room, wringing his hands.

My back straightens, fear overtaking me. "Whatever you're thinking, stop. Let's get cleaned up and talk."

After getting dressed, he hands me a glass of water and we go to sit at his dining room table. Why does it feel like there's something big that I've missed?

"Ada, how much do you know about orcs?"

"Well, I know a bit, but I wouldn't call myself an expert," I say, giving a nervous laugh. My romance book research and late night online searches probably don't count for much.

"Orcs aren't like humans. Not to state the obvious. But we aren't just physically different from humans, we're also different in the way that we find partners. Humans date as many people as they'd like, possibly settle down, or settle down with various people throughout their lives. Orcs...we can't do that. We are biologically made to find our one true fated mate."

"Okay...That much I do know." Where is he going with this? Did he find his fated mate and doesn't want to see me anymore?

"Once an orc meets their fated mate, they'll do anything to win them over. Primal urges from our ancestors start kicking in. Their mate will be the one and only love of their life for as long as they both live," he shares, his tone growing serious. "No one else will do, but their mate."

"How does an orc know that they've found their mate?" This was the one thing I never thought about, but should have.

"To start with, there's the scenting," he says. "Our mates give off an almost addicting scent that's uniquely appealing to each orc. We also sense the bond on a soul-deep level. It's like the final puzzle piece has fallen into place. Your mate fills your every thought, and you only feel whole when you're with them. A mating bond is permanent and once it's accepted, it's forever. That kind of love is something young orcs dream of finding." His eyes gleam with unshed tears.

"Ulgan, why are you telling me this?" I ask, my stomach twisting in knots. "Have you met your fated mate?"

"Sunshine, *you're* my mate."

fourteen
ada

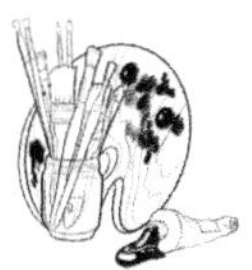

All of the breath leaves my lungs at his confession. *His mate.* Is this why I feel so drawn to him? Do humans feel the mating bond too?

"Excuse me, *what*?" I say.

I look over at him, and his gaze doesn't waver. "Ada, please hear me out. I won't pressure you into anything if this isn't something you're interested in exploring. You have all the power here, Sunshine."

I try to let his words sink in, but my mind is racing. "How long have you known?" According to him and my research, an orc knows almost instantly when they've encountered their mate.

So why didn't he tell me?

"I knew that you were my fated mate from the first time you walked into the bakery. You took my breath away the moment I laid eyes on you," Ulgan says. "The last thing I wanted to do was scare you or make you feel like you were trapped. That's why I didn't say anything. I wanted you to get to know me, and hoped that one day you'd give me a chance to show you why the Goddess made us for one another."

This is overwhelming to take in. My feelings for him have grown with each passing day while getting to know him, but what if this is all just a load of crap? There's no way that this thing growing between us is real. It's probably just the mating bond making him feel this way. No one has ever wanted something serious with me. I am always someone that's okay for a short period of time, but not anyone that men have taken seriously.

A guy that I was seeing years ago told me that I was only good for a little fun and that no man would ever want to settle down with someone like me. I want Ulgan to be my forever, but it's hard to believe he wants the same. I fucking hate that I feel this way.

"I have deep feelings for you, Ulgan, but it's hard for me to accept that you'd want me forever. People in my life have a habit of leaving, and if you were to leave me, I don't think I could ever recover." My voice trembles, and I can feel the panic settling in.

Ulgan reaches for my shaking hands across the table, gently holding them. "Ada, please know that I'm not going anywhere. I've waited months for you, but I'm willing to wait years if it means you'll believe in what we have. I'm falling for you hard and fast, Sunshine, but you're in charge now. What do you need from me to feel more comfortable?"

It kills me to say it, but the one thing I need is time to think. His reasoning for not telling me makes sense, but it still leaves a nasty taste in my mouth.

"I need some space to think this through. Please, you need to know that this isn't a *no*," I insist. "I'm falling for you, too, but I need to sort through my feelings. I want to believe you. I really do, but it's so hard to wrap my head around. Can you give me time?"

My heart breaks as the words leave my lips. Part of me knows that Ulgan isn't like other men that have mistreated me, but another part still holds onto the pain and heartbreak from my past.

He gets up from his chair, and I find myself standing as well. "Is it okay if I give you a hug?" he asks hesitantly. Words are stuck in my throat, but I'm able to nod. He brings me into his arms, kissing the top of my head. I linger in his warm embrace until my heart stutters. "Take all the time you need. Just know this: I'm not going anywhere, and I'll be here when you decide how you want to move forward."

He gives me a brief kiss on the lips, and walks me to the door. "Goodnight, Ada."

"Goodnight, Ulgan."

The walk home is a blur. All my fears swirl around me like ghosts from my past, haunting me in the present. These old scars of mine feel like fresh wounds. Clearly, my habit of shoving difficult feelings deep down and not addressing them has led me to this exact moment.

Angeline has been trying to convince me to speak to a therapist for over a year now, but I've been afraid to open that Pandora's box. Now, it's evident that she could see the pain that I tried so desperately to hide.

On one hand, I'm thankful that he finally told me, but on the other hand, it triggered fears I thought I had healed from. Dammit, I hate feeling broken. Not even bothering to change my clothes, I climb into bed and let myself release the tears that I'd been holding in.

Did I just ruin everything between him and me? Ulgan isn't like the other men I've dated. He's loving and respects me and my decisions. He made sure that I knew I was in control. Maybe a good night's sleep will allow me to think clearly. Salty tears burn my eyes as I lay in bed wondering what to do.

fifteen
ulgan

Watching Ada walk down those stairs tonight feels like my world is crashing in on me. I just went from having the best night of my life to the worst in a matter of minutes. The look of shock and fear on her face once she learned that we were mates felt like a sucker punch to the gut. This is all my fault. If only I'd told her sooner, or maybe not at all.

No, she deserved to know the truth. But not like this.

After pacing my apartment for the hundredth time, it feels like the walls close in on me. I need to get the hell out of here and clear my head. I grab my coat and head outside, hoping that the fresh air will do something to change how shitty I feel. After wandering aimlessly downtown for over an hour, my feet lead me back through the woods to my workshop.

Tonight is a nightmare that I need to wake the fuck up from. How did everything crash and burn like that? My worst fear was realized. I admitted my feelings to Ada and now I've scared her and ruined everything that we could've had.

Dammit, why did I have to call her "mate"? I was trying to give her time to warm up to the idea, and instead I had to open my big mouth.

Frustration and self-loathing war within me. Grabbing my ax from the workbench, I walk over to my pile of wood that's meant for future projects. Well, fuck that. I need to blow off some steam, and this wood is about to be the target of my frustrations. I indiscriminately land blow after blow on every block of wood in my proximity. Each blow is accompanied by loud roars of anguish.

A short while later, my muscles are burning and my breath is labored. A massive pile of chopped wood sits next to me. Placing another hunk of wood on the chopping stump, my arms shake as I raise the ax above my head. A guttural grunt leaves my chest as the head of the ax connects with the wood.

Sitting down on the beaten-up stump, I close my eyes and try to get my breathing under control. Exhaustion wins in the end, and after putting my ax back in the shop, I trudge up the stairs to my apartment. Removing my shoes, my body collapses onto my bed. Things can't get much worse than today, right?

I'm so screwed.

Early the following morning, my head is pounding, and all I want to do is crawl under a rock. Instead, I take some pain relievers and head downstairs to open the shop for the day. My phone rings again for the fifth time this morning, and after a quick glance, I see that it's Theo. I don't have the energy to talk to anyone right now. Turning my phone off, I get back to adding more cupcakes to the display case when the bell above the door rings.

"Welcome to Blissful Bites, I'll be right with you in a moment," I say, not looking up from the case.

"What the hell, dude? Why are you ignoring my calls?" Theo

shouts. "Did I interrupt something between you and your mate this morning?" He turns the *Open* sign on the door to *Closed,* and sits down at one of the small white metal tables that I have for customers who want to stay and eat. Joining him, my body sags against the back of the too-small chair and my face can't hide how crappy I feel.

His playful demeanor becomes serious. "Oh shit, what happened?"

What didn't go wrong?

"I fucked up big time and accidentally called her my mate." My head falls into my hands that I have propped on the table.

I lift my head in time to see Theo's eyes widen, and his mouth opens like he's going to say something but thinks better of it.

"Go ahead, tell me how badly I messed this whole thing up." My head hangs and eyes close, waiting for him to let me know how I destroyed my chance at happiness.

"I'm assuming by your reaction that she didn't take it well?" he asks, trying to keep his voice calm for me.

"I scared the shit out of her. She said that she needed time to think about it. The night was going so well, too," I say, trying and failing to keep how hurt I am from seeping into my voice.

"Let me just get this straight. You had an amazing evening with your beautiful mate, and slipped up and called her your mate—which she is. Am I right so far?" he asks.

"Yep." I'm such an idiot.

"And she seemed a little freaked out, and asked for space to think?" he clarifies again.

"Spot on." It hasn't even been twenty-four hours and her absence is already killing me.

"Ulgan, relax. This doesn't mean that the night was ruined. It just means that your very human mate needs time to process something that's not normal where she comes from. If the rest of the evening was going well, then it probably isn't as bad as you think it is."

Shaking my head, I can't help but disagree. He wasn't there to see the shock on her face or how quickly she wanted to get away from me.

"It's time to call in reinforcements." Theo pulls out his phone and dials.

"Little witch, I need a favor."

Is he talking to who I *think* he's talking to?

"Yes, I'm aware that you think I'm a *The LOTR* reject, but I have a hurt orc here who needs some answers. Yes, fine, I'll owe you one. We're at the bakery right now. How quick can you get here?"

Is Rue coming here? Would she be able to shed some light on what happened last night?

"Are you seriously giving me your coffee order right now? Little witch, you are playing a dangerous game. Okay, see you soon. Bye, Rue." Yelling could be heard from the other side of the phone before Theo hangs up. "Rue's on her way."

A few minutes later, the witch herself walks into the bakery with a scowl on her face, but it disappears once she sees me. "Oh shit. What happened?" She moves to the table, turning a chair around and sitting on it backwards. "Ulgan, did you do something to hurt my best friend? Am I going to have to kill you?" Her eyes narrow at me.

Theo quickly explains what happened, and I chime in to fill in the blanks whenever she asks a question. Her eyes soften.

Rue looks like she's contemplating how to phrase her words, and after a long sigh, she says, "Everything that I'm about to tell you needs to stay between us or else you'll wake up bald tomorrow. Oh, and elf boy, I'm going to need that coffee now."

Theo rolls his eyes and gets up from the chair to make her a cup of coffee. He tries to hide his smirk, but I caught it. These two just need to get together already.

Rue turns back to me. "Okay, proceed," she says, gesturing for me to spit it out.

Here it goes. "I'm in love with her, Rue. Please, I need to know how to fix this."

She takes a deep breath and releases another heavy sigh. "Ulgan, you didn't do anything wrong other than keeping a secret from her. Ada's not really big on secrets. You have to stop beating yourself up, though. Has Ada shared anything about her past with you?"

"She told me about her parents and grandmother passing away, but not much else."

"Ada's life hasn't been easy. She was left to fend for herself by the age of eighteen. So, she's used to being alone. Then, the assholes she dated treated her like she wasn't worthy of anything serious. She hasn't admitted it, but she tends to think that relationships and friendships are just temporary. That one day we'll disappear from her life, too. She truly believes that there's no way that anyone would want to be with her for the long haul."

"I would never do that to her." Knowing this is how she feels, my heart breaks. My poor Sunshine. No wonder she panicked the way she did. I need her to understand that I'm not going anywhere, and that she's the only woman that my heart will ever love and desire.

Theo returns with Rue's coffee, placing it in front of her before sitting down again.

"Of course you wouldn't hurt her, big guy," Rue takes a small sip of her coffee. "She just needs some time to stop being so in her head and realize that for herself. Give Ada the space she asked for, and I'll work some magic on my end."

I've known Rue since we were kids, and her compassion for others has always been something that I admire. She may have a tough exterior, but on the inside, she's a softie. I'll *never* tell her this though, because she kind of scares me.

"Okay, I'll give her space, but what if it doesn't work, and she never wants to see me again?" The thought of never being around her again is unbearable. The dull ache in my chest has become a tight fist clenching around my heart.

"I know my bestie. She's just as smitten as you are. So be patient, okay?" She reaches across the table and places her hand on top of mine.

"All right. Thanks for talking to me, Rue. You're an incredible woman." Give her time and space. I can do that. It'll suck, but it's manageable.

"No problem, Big Green. As for you," she says, pointing at Theo, "I'll be sure to call in that favor one day when you least expect it."

That sounds vaguely like a threat. Theo better watch himself.

"I look forward to that day, little witch." His arms are crossed against his chest, and he's smirking at her in a way that I wouldn't dare to do.

"See you around, bootleg Legolas." Rue turns on her heels and marches out of the bakery.

"Bootleg Legolas?" My eyebrows rise, looking over at Theo.

"You gotta give her points for creativity," he remarks, still grinning, and his eyes linger on Rue.

sixteen
ada

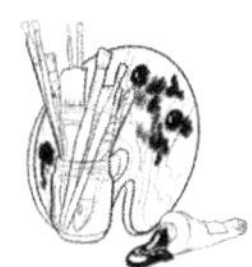

My attempt to relax on the couch backfires. I find it almost impossible to get comfortable. My breath becomes labored as self-doubt and dark, ugly feelings, feelings I thought were long dead and buried, bubble to the surface. Ulgan's confession last night made my heart soar, then plummet to the ground. My feelings for him have grown quickly, and that scares the shit out of me.

Picking up my phone, I dial Rue's number, as the room closes in on me. Finally, she picks up on the third ring. "Hey, babe."

The dam breaks. No longer able to hold back the tears that'd been carefully locked away, panicked sobs overwhelm my body. "Rue, I need you." I'm barely able to get the words out.

A short time later the front door opens and Rue rushes in, pulling me close. "You need to breathe, babe. Cry all you want, but remember to breathe."

Eventually the sobs subside. Rue brushes my hair. "Can you tell me what happened?"

Wiping away my tears, it's time to finally say out loud what caused me to break down.

Rue listens intently as I explain to her what happened with Ulgan the night before.

"I'm going to be honest with you, okay? We have no secrets between us. I saw Ulgan this morning already."

I immediately feel like crying again. She has?

"How is he?" Guilt claws at me, waiting for her to speak.

"He looks about as bad as you do right now."

I did that to him. My fucked up head ruined the best thing that's ever happened to me.

"Can I ask something?" Rue asks. I nod, giving her the okay, but now I'm finding it difficult to look her in the eyes.

"You've been through so much loss in your life, and that's made you think that people and relationships are moments away from disappearing."

"Is there a question in there?" I say, feeling defensive for having my deepest fear exposed. Fuck, I hate feeling vulnerable like this.

She reaches over, holding both of my hands in hers. "Do you think that I'm temporary?"

Of course not. Rue is the best friend I've ever had. We've been through the highs and lows of life together, and she's always been there. Rue's the sister that I had always dreamed of growing up.

"No. Absolutely not."

"Okay, we're getting somewhere," she says. "What about Mom? Or Hannah? Or Isla? They each love you fiercely. Do you think that they are all temporary in your life? Do you really think that they'll disappear one day too?"

All of them have shown me more love and acceptance than

anyone outside of Mom, Dad, and Granny. "No. None of you are temporary."

"Do you truly, deep down in your heart, believe that Ulgan will wake up one morning and just leave? Obviously, I haven't been following you two around like a creep, but it's clear to anyone who has spent a second with the both of you that there's love between you. Not just short term infatuation like those gross teenagers that you see making out at the mall. What you and Ulgan have is soul deep. It's one of those loves that you read about in your book porn."

Rue's words flow through me, easing some of my earlier feelings, but the scared and lonely little girl in me still needs some time to process everything. The mere idea of being Ulgan's mate conjures images of a future filled with love, acceptance, and joy. Giving in and accepting that could mean that it all gets taken away from me. First, my parents and grandmother. Could I handle another loss? Is it worth the risk?

"I hear you, but I need time to clear my mind and sort through how I'm feeling."

"That's understandable. How about I get out of here and give you some time alone? Be forewarned that I'm coming back tomorrow if I don't hear from you." She gets up from her spot next to me and strolls right out the front door.

As always, she's right. I need to do something instead of just sitting here feeling like crap. Setting up my painting supplies, I get to work. With each brush stroke, the chaos within my mind is nowhere near ready to settle.

This has become a routine of mine. Whenever life was too much for me to handle, painting helped to bring me back to myself. The walls of my cottage are now adorned with what I lovingly call my, 'Holy-fuck-I'm-stressed creations.' Radiant flowers of all kinds, little fairy villages, and other fantasy scenes can be found adorning every available surface. The sun begins to set before I notice that the day has gotten away from me. Putting the finishing touches on the miniature mushrooms above the bathroom light switch, it's evident that I was far more overwhelmed than I thought.

My stomach is growling at me to feed it. After a quick meal of leftovers, there's no energy left in my body to do anything other than sleep. Painting today helped to physically calm me down, but my mind is still a mess. Hopefully some rest will help me to make sense of the warring feelings inside.

In the morning, I'm ripped from my sleep by a loud banging on my front door. Throwing on my robe, I march to find the asshole that woke me up. Rubbing the crud from my eyes, and opening the door, I'm nearly run over by Rue as she barges her way into the house.

"You've added some new additions to the walls, I see." She walks over to the closed living room curtains and whips them open. I throw a hand up to cover my eyes. "Enough moping, it's time that you and I had a conversation. Take a seat, and I'll get some tea ready." Two steaming cups of tea appear on the coffee table in front of us, and we sit down on the couch. "Have you eaten yet this morning? No, you probably haven't. Now, you eat that and just listen to what I have to say," she says, pointing to a plate that has a mouthwatering eggs benedict and a heaping pile of shredded hashbrowns on it.

There are many reasons why I love Rue, and her ability to conjure me eggs benny is certainly one of them.

"Did you have a chance to think about what I said?" she asks, staring me down.

"Yes. You're right." Wow, that's hard to admit.

"I always am, but could you be more specific?"

This bitch...

"I *do* worry that everyone in my life is going to leave. I'm afraid that there's something wrong with me that makes people not want to stick around. Obviously, my family didn't purposefully do it, but there's a part of me that's pissed that I spent so much time feeling alone. It's something that I need to work on, and now I'm terrified that I ruined things with Ulgan because of it." Getting that off my chest makes me feel one thousand pounds lighter. Angeline was right, I do need to talk to someone about my grief.

"What are you going to do now? What does *Ada* want to do right now?" Rue asks.

I've let my past dictate my future for far too long. It's up to me to ensure that I have the future that I deserve, with a partner that will love me unconditionally, and allows me to do the same.

"I need to go." I push myself up and speed toward the front door, only stopping to give Rue a quick hug. I need to go find him!

"Go get your man!" Rue shouts from the open door as I make my way toward the bakery. Of course, I was so focused on leaving that I forgot my umbrella. Heavy rain falls from the sky in sheets, soaking through my sweatshirt, making me shiver. I pull open the door to the bakery and head over to the counter, ringing the service bell probably one too many times. Benji pokes his head around the corner.

"Hi Ada, I'll be with you in one moment."

"Benji, is Ulgan here? I need to speak to him." I should be embarrassed that I sound so frantic, but I don't care anymore.

"The boss isn't here right now, but he should be upstairs at his place," he says, giving me a curious look.

"Thank you!" I turn and run from the shop to the back

staircase. Climbing the stairs two at a time, I'm out of breath by the time I reach the top and knock on the door insistently.

It slowly opens, and standing in front of me is a statuesque and gorgeous orc woman around my age. She looks familiar, and it takes me a moment to remember where I've seen her before.

"Hi, can I help you?" she asks, her brows furrow as I stand there panting. She brushes her long black hair out of her face to get a better look at me.

"Um, is Ulgan here? Can you tell him that Ada needs to speak to him?" I must look like a soaked cat, rain still pouring down on me.

"You're Ada?" Her eyes grow wide with recognition. "Ulgan!" she shouts into the apartment. She turns back to me, placing her arm around my back to guide me inside. "Come in and get out of the rain. I'm Ulgan's sister, Selene. I've been dying to meet you." Her joy is written all over her face.

Finally getting a good look at her, I realize that Selene is basically a supermodel. She's one of those girls who would look chic in anything she wears. She's currently wearing an oversized sweatshirt and bike shorts, and looks like she just stepped out of a magazine photoshoot.

"What are you shouting for?" Ulgan says, sounding annoyed coming out of his bedroom. I'm currently hidden behind his much taller sister. Selene moves to the side, revealing me, and Ulgan is unable to hide the surprise on his face. Those beautiful eyes of his light up when he spots me.

"Ada," he whispers, making his way to me slowly, as if he's afraid he'll startle me. I must *really* look like a soaked cat if he thinks he'll startle me. "Love, what are you doing here? You're soaking wet. Come with me so we can get you dried off." He places his arm around my shoulders, and we start to make our way to his bedroom when a musical voice sounds behind us.

"Ulgie, I know that you aren't going to rush past me without introducing me to your friend."

Ulgie? Well, if that isn't the cutest nickname.

"Mom, this is Ada. Ada, this is my mother, Edie. Mom, you can get to know her better once I have her in some warm clothes."

Edie is so freaking cute.

She's much smaller than Ulgan and Selene, but still towers over me. The radiant older orc is wearing a charming pink floral dress with a cream cardigan resting over her shoulders. Her gray hair is pulled back into a long neat braid.

"Hurry back, Ulgie. Ada and I are going to be fast friends, I can just tell." I quickly wave to her, as he ushers me into his bedroom.

This is my first time in his bedroom, and the nosy part of me looks around quickly. His bed is gigantic, taking up most of the room. It's covered with a light gray comforter that works well with the cream colored walls and light wood furniture. I wouldn't be surprised if he made all of this furniture himself.

Closing the door behind him, he spins, eyes landing on me. In my eagerness to get here, I didn't actually think about what I would actually say once I saw him.

"Dammit, I missed you," he says, trying to pull me toward him.

Placing my hands on his chest I stop him. "I don't want to get you wet." What am I even saying? Being in his arms is the only place I want to be.

"Fuck that. I don't care about a little water, I just need to hold you." We stand holding on to one another in silence. Placing my head on his chest, he rests his chin on top of my head, breathing me in.

Lifting my head, I muster all of the bravery I can. "Ulgan, I'm so sorry about the other night. I was overwhelmed, and it was unfair of me to leave the way I did. You shouldn't have to pay for what others have done to me. I'm so sorry." I almost let this incredible man slip through my fingers.

It's then I notice that tears are streaming down my face. In an instant, his callused thumbs are on my cheeks, brushing them away. His eyes shine with unshed tears of his own.

"Ada, you have nothing to apologize for. Orcs are raised understanding how fated mates work. It's a lot for you to process, and I never want you to feel rushed. My hope is that one day you'll give me the chance to earn your love," he says.

"That's the thing though, you've already got it." I love him. I love Ulgan Durzum so much, and it feels amazing to finally admit it to myself.

"Sunshine, what are you saying? Please, love. Please, give me the words."

"I love you, Ulgan. You're my mate, and I'm yours," I say in between sobs.

"You're mine?" he asks, uncertainty still lingering between us.

"Yes, Ulgan. I'm yours. I'm all yours, if you'll still have me."

Please. Please don't say that it's too late.

"Thank Goddess." He quickly pulls me closer to him again and kisses me, except this isn't some sweet kiss like before. This is a kiss filled with longing and desperation. He devours my mouth like a thirsty man who's finally been given a drink. He places kisses across my face, starting at my cheeks, before moving to the bridge of my nose, and eyelids. "I love you with everything that I am, Ada. You are everything that I thought I would never have. I love you so much, Sunshine."

His declaration makes me feel lighter than air. He lifts me in his strong arms, and my legs wrap around his waist. He presses my body against the back of the door, going back to devouring my mouth.

His lips return to mine, but before we can go any further, there's a knock on his bedroom door.

"Ulgan, are the two of you almost done in there?" his mother's voice asks sweetly from the other side.

My hands fly to cover my mouth. "Could they hear us?" I whisper from behind my hands, mortified.

Before he can respond, his mother shouts, "Yes dear, but don't you worry, we're leaving."

Okay, it's official. This is easily the most embarrassing thing that's ever happened to me. I wouldn't mind if the earth opened up and swallowed me whole right now.

Ulgan's hand rests on my cheek, forcing me to look at him. "It's going to be okay. Let's get you some dry clothes and go out there, but this is far from over. Once they're gone, you are mine."

My core clenches on nothing, and I silently curse that we aren't alone. The primal way he said "*mine*" has flames of desire coursing through my veins. He hands me a dry t-shirt and a pair of shorts that are far too big. He helps me roll the shorts so they don't fall down. Then, I realize I can't stall anymore. It's time to face his family.

seventeen
ada

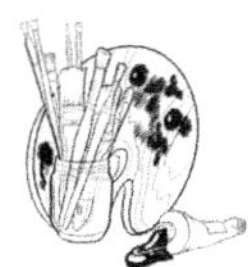

We exit the bedroom and find Selene forcing Edie into her coat, trying to usher her outside. Selene turns around briefly to address us. "Ada, welcome to the family! We'll see the two of you tomorrow. Say goodbye, Mom."

"Goodnight, you two!" Edie waves over her shoulder before Selene rushes her outside and the door closes behind them.

Ulgan and I are left standing in his kitchen, tension thick between us. He gives a low growl before stalking toward me like a predator after his prey. I am *very* willing prey.

Finally standing before me, he shocks the shit out of me when I'm lifted off my feet and placed on the kitchen counter. Ulgan and I are now eye to eye, and he leans in to bury his face into my neck. He nuzzles me like a content house cat, his nostrils flaring against my sensitive skin. My breathing picks up as my eyes slowly close. Suddenly, Ulgan runs his tongue along the length of my neck, giving a breathy moan in my ear.

My arms snake around his back, pulling him closer to me.

Having a mind of their own, my hips begin to move, grinding against Ulgan's firm stomach.

He pulls back and shoots me a lopsided grin. "Is my little mate needy right now?"

A soft moan falls from my lips. "Yes."

That's all it takes to make Ulgan snap. My usually sweet and awkward mate reaches toward me and rips the shirt I'm wearing in half, exposing my bare breasts to him. It's the sexiest thing that's ever happened to me.

"Your shirt needs to go," I say. My arms reach to tug his shirt over his head. There's no way I'm having a barrier between us right now. My hands explore his wide muscular chest, taking my time running my hands over the light sprinkling of hair. His chest rapidly rises and falls as he tries to keep himself in control, and I freaking love that he's having a hard time doing it. My hands travel down his slightly soft stomach and head further south, before he snatches both of my wrists in one of his much larger hands.

"Enough teasing. I need to taste you. Take. Those. Off. Now." His voice is deep and thick with want. This more dominant side of Ulgan has me almost coming from his voice alone.

"These are only coming off if your pants come off, too." My bratty-ass self needs to see him naked.

Ulgan slowly backs up from the counter, and then quickly pulls down his pants and briefs. "You better get those off now, or I'm ripping them too."

Shooting him a mischievous smile, I run my hands over my covered pussy, teasing him. "But, what if I want you to rip them off?" Lightning fast, he's on me, and my panties are torn from my body. The scraps float down to the floor.

Ulgan goes back to kissing my neck, alternating between kisses and sinful nips. Working his way down my collarbone, he covers every inch with soft strokes of his tongue. His hands smooth over my thighs, getting tantalizingly closer to the place where I want him the most. My head rests against a cabinet door behind me as I luxuriate under his attention.

"Baby, please, I need more." I'm not too proud to beg right now.

"Let me take care of you, mate." His mouth lowers to one of my bare breasts, and he places a light kiss to my aching nipple.

I suck in a breath. Ulgan's tongue swirls around my nipple, while his other hand massages my other breast. My nipple is sucked fully into his mouth as he moans like he can't contain himself. His teeth lightly scrape my skin, and I can feel my pussy dripping onto the counter, making a mess.

"Touch me." Oh, I can do that. My arms shoot out and grab his shoulders to anchor myself. He moves on, worshiping my other breast as I pant and chant my love for him over and over.

He leaves one final kiss on my breast, and scatters kisses down my stomach and runs his tongue over my stretch marks. Fuck, so this is what it feels like to be treasured?

"Mmmm, is my little mate ready for me to taste her?" He looks up from between my legs at me.

"Please, Ulgan. I need to cum so badly. It hurts." My body is on fire and I need to feel his tongue on my clit.

"I'll take care of you, my love." His large warm hands rub my thighs and then spread them wider to accommodate his large frame.

He inhales my scent deep into his lungs and his eyes become hooded. Ulgan eats me like I'm a fucking feast. His broad tongue laps at me over and over again. A scream leaves me as he gives a satisfied groan against my core. The vibrations are driving me wild, and pushing me closer to the edge.

"Ulgan, I'm so close. Please." I need to come *now*.

He must have heard the desperation in my voice because he immediately starts circling my clit before firmly sucking it between his lips. My back arches and suddenly I'm coming hard, my body convulsing as Ulgan licks me through my orgasm. He continues showering attention on my overly sensitive clit, and I have to push his face away.

"Baby, it's too much." I need a break after his attention. He kisses my inner thighs before standing back up. My cum glistens on his chin and I can't help but lean in and lick it off. He grabs the back of my neck and pulls me into a deep kiss as our tongues fight for dominance. I pull back, kissing his neck. "Ulgan, that was incredible. You make me feel so good."

"Oh, I'm not done with you yet, Sunshine." Thank fucking Goddess for that! He lifts me up, cradles me to his chest and carries me to his bedroom. I'm gently lowered onto the plush oversized bed, and he crawls up my body, resting his weight on his arms. "You are the most beautiful woman that I've ever seen. Every inch of you is perfect." My heart skips a beat. Little does he know how much he's healing my heart by saying that.

"Ulgan, I need you inside of me. I feel so empty." My desperation has hit an all time high.

"Shh. You want my cock, love? Does my mate need her orc to fill up her needy little pussy?" he whispers to me, nipping at my earlobe.

"I need you now. Please don't make me wait any longer." I need to feel him.

"Ada." His voice has a touch of seriousness to it. "Love, I need you to let me know if I'm too rough, okay? It would devastate me if I hurt you. Also, the suppressants I'm on prevent pregnancy, so we don't need to worry about that right now."

"Ulgan, I'll let you know if you do anything I don't like. Thank you for telling me about the suppressants. I don't want to get pregnant right now, but I also don't want anything between us. Now, please fuck me."

Ulgan moves his hand between my legs, stroking my clit with his talented fingers.

"Fuck, love, you're so wet for me." He abandons my clit and grips his length, guiding the tip toward my core.

Slowly, he begins to enter me before pulling back and starting over again. He's letting me get used to his size, and the stretch is indescribable. The thick ridges on either side of his cock rub me in just the right way as he thrusts in and out.

Finally, he gives one last thrust and he's fully seated inside of me. "Sunshine, your pussy grips me so well. Oh Goddess, your body is driving me crazy."

"I'm so fucking full." I'm panting, trying to catch my breath.

"Are you okay? Do you need me to slow down?" he asks, sounding worried. I love that he cares so deeply about making this a good experience for me.

"I'm more than okay. You feel incredible inside of me." I clench my core around his length and his head snaps back.

He looks back down at me, lust reflecting back in his eyes. His hands grip my waist and he begins to thrust faster. His hips piston back and forth, our combined cries of ecstasy fill the room. We're both drenched with sweat as we chase an orgasm. Something firm presses against my pussy as he moves in and out of me.

This must be his knot. He already warned me about it, and

I've done my own independent research on the matter. Purely for scientific reasons, of course. This knot is going to stretch me to my limits and it honestly makes me a little nervous. I'm already stuffed full.

"Ulgan, baby. Can we wait for your knot?" I pant, trying to get the words out. My breasts are firmly pressed to his damp chest, fingers clutching at his back and leaving red nail marks behind.

"Ada, look at me." Our eyes meet and there is so much love swimming in his chocolate brown eyes. "We can wait until you're ready for my knot. There's no rush, Sunshine. We have our entire lives to explore that. Now, let me make love to you."

Relief washes over me at his words. Ulgan continues rocking into me until we both come hard, his seed shooting into me in thick spurts.

We hold each other through the aftershocks and stay wrapped in each other's arms for some time after. His head drops, using my breasts as a pillow, and my arms wrap around his back, rubbing his fatigued shoulders.

"I love you so much, Sunshine," he says, nuzzling my breasts and placing soft kisses on them.

"I love you too, Ulgan. Forever."

LAST NIGHT CHANGED everything between Ulgan and I. Waking up this morning, it takes me a moment to realize where I am. The soft comforter on top of me smells exactly like Ulgan, and it's addictive. Holding the comforter to my nose, I breathe in that rich masculine scent that I love. It's then that I notice the warm body pressed against my back, and the heavy arm wrapped around my waist. My mate's arm pulls me tighter to his chest. I begin to wonder if he's still asleep until I feel gentle kisses on my bare shoulder and hear a low satisfied moan.

A giggle bursts from me. Ulgan buries his head between my shoulder and neck, leaving loud wet kisses there. "Mmmm," he moans again into my ear. "I love the sound of your laughter."

He pulls back just enough so I'm able to turn around and face him. Reaching up, I caress him, allowing my fingertips to trace over every part of his beautiful face. "Good morning." My voice sounds sleepy still.

"It is a good morning indeed, mate." Inching closer to him, I place my hands on his chest and rest my head on top to look in his eyes. One of my fingers lazily traces the tattoos covering his chest.

"How are you feeling this morning?" he asks, wrapping his arms around my back and caressing me with his rough palms. I could cum again just from him touching me like this. My vagina needs to calm the hell down for a second.

Ulgan and I made love over and over again last night, falling asleep for short periods of time only to wake up and do it all over again.

"A bit sore, but the best kind of sore," I say with a satisfied smirk.

"I wasn't too rough?" He voices his worry again.

"Last night was the best night of my life. I loved every single thing that we did, and I plan on doing it again very soon."

His laugh makes my heart skip a beat. "How about we take a shower and have some breakfast. Hopefully that'll alleviate any soreness in your muscles so you can get a repeat performance tonight."

My core weeps, so freaking excited already.

We make our way to the bathroom and decide to conserve water by showering together. Gotta save the planet, you know? It had nothing to do with the fact that Ulgan got me all hot and bothered again by strutting his fine ass in front of me as we stepped into the shower. Not that he complained. My man has made it clear that he loves every single inch of my body.

Ulgan squirts some shower gel into his hands, then rubs them together under the water for it to lather. The mouthwatering scent of pine and leather that I've come to associate with him fills the small space. He then takes those sexy as fuck hands and helps to 'clean' me. What started out as innocent, or as innocent as running your hands all over someone's body can be, quickly becomes something more when he reaches my aching breasts.

Palms cupping each breast, Ulgan massages them with light squeezes before focusing his attention on my still tender nipples. Last night, Ulgan worshiped my breasts thoroughly, so I guess it's safe to say that he appreciates them.

He rubs each nipple with his thumbs before giving them a light pinch and tug. His hands leave my breasts and grip my hips as he turns me to face him. My poor well-loved pussy needs a little break, so I decide to give him my best sultry smile before lowering myself to kneel on the wet tile.

Ulgan's cock is my new best friend. Sorry, Rue, but this big fella has claimed the number one spot. I'm making it my personal mission to memorize each and every glorious inch of his dick.

"Ulgan?" There's something I need him to do for me, and I hope that he agrees.

"Yes, love?" He gazes down at me, heat and love in his eyes.

"Can you call me your good little mate again? When you did it last night it really turned me on."

"Oh, Sunshine I am more than happy to oblige. Now, suck my cock like the good little mate that you are."

Thank goddess we're in the shower already or I'd be a wet mess. Not needing any further encouragement, my eyes drift down to my new bestie bobbing in front of me. It was time to show my man what a good mate I could be.

My tongue starts at the base of him and I slowly lick my way up to the tip. On instinct, Ulgan's hands twist into my hair, holding me to him.

"Oh shit, sorry Ada." He sounds embarrassed, but I freaking loved it.

"Don't you dare let go of my hair." I resume licking him up and down before sucking the tip into my mouth and running my tongue over his leaking slit. His distinctive cinnamon cum is addictive, and the second it hits my tastebuds I can't hold back my moan.

"Oh fuck, your mouth feels so fucking good. Be a good little mate and suck me down further."

He doesn't have to ask me twice. Ulgan is huge, so I'm only able to fit some of him into my mouth, but I make up for it by massaging him as I alternate between licking and sucking.

"That's it, love. I'm so close. Oh fuck! Almost there, yes, you're such a good fucking mate for me aren't you?"

Moments later, Ulgan's delicious cum hits the back of my throat and I greedily drink him down. My hands and tongue continue to work him as his orgasm makes him shake. His fingers tighten in my hair when he comes, but I don't mind. He releases me and leans against the shower wall.

"Holy shit," he says breathlessly. "I imagined you doing this very thing to me in the shower." A playful smirk spreads across my lips. Very interesting.

"I'd be more than happy to bring any other fantasies you've had about me to life." I try to sound innocent, but my inner sex goddess is at full force right now.

His cock twitches at my words. "Fuck, you're incredible." We both laugh, and I rest my head on his thigh.

Ulgan regains his strength, picking me up to kiss me deeply. I'm happy I can do this for him. The fact that little old me brought him that much pleasure satisfies me like nothing else.

We finish showering, and Ulgan helps to dry my body off and gives me one of his t-shirts to wear. The shirt falls to my knees and is more like a dress, but wearing his clothes and being wrapped in his scent makes my heart happy.

I wander from his bedroom to the kitchen, where I find him in a pair of gray sweatpants and no shirt as he brews coffee in his fancy looking coffee maker.

"I'm sorry, but you have no right to look this damn sexy this early in the morning," I say, walking over to him and wrapping my arms around his large muscular waist. I rest my head on his bare back, and my naughty fingers stroke over his stomach, giving extra attention to his yummy muscles. "Are you aware that gray sweatpants are every woman's kryptonite?"

"No, but I'd be more than happy to wear them as often as you'd like," he says, his back straightening with confidence.

We eat breakfast and it feels like something we've done for years. Ulgan checks on his supply order on his phone while I finish up lesson plans on his laptop. Every now and then he leans over to give me a quick peck or hold my hand in his.

A knock on the door disrupts our little domestic bliss. Ulgan goes to the front door and lets out a groan when he sees who it is.

His large body blocks my view, but there's no mistaking the owner of the sweet voice. "Good morning, my favorite son!"

"Mom, I'm your only son."

"Well, you're my favorite." She peers around Ulgan and waves to me. I'm frozen at the kitchen table, trying to pull his shirt further down my body so she can't see that I'm wearing nothing underneath it. "Good morning, Ada! How's my new daughter doing this lovely morning?"

I wave back at her. "Good morning, Edie."

"Now, Ulgie, let your mother in. Are you really going to make me stand out here?" Ulgan doesn't budge an inch.

"You know that I love you, mom, but I need some time alone with my mate," he groans.

"I know that, but it's not every day that a mother's son finally meets his fated mate. Just a few minutes?" I can't see the look on Ulgan's face, but clearly he is not pleased. "Oh, okay! I can take a hint. But I expect to see the two of you at my house for dinner at some point this week. No excuses, young man."

Ulgan roars with laughter and gives his mother a hug. "I love you, Ma. We'll see you soon."

"Bye, Ada dear! We should go out to lunch together soon with Selene, since she's in town. It's been ages since I've had a little girl-time."

I have a feeling that Edie and I are going to become fast friends.

"I would love that. See you later!" We wave to each other as she peers around Ulgan's large frame again.

He closes the door and drops back into his seat next to me. "Sorry about that, Sunshine. I swear, she's amazing, but damn can she meddle."

Getting up from my chair, I move to sit in his lap, and I love how well we fit together. Being in his arms already feels like home, and I let out a contented sigh as he holds me close.

"Oh, I forgot to ask you earlier," I say, "but would you like to be my date to an event at Rue's place next week for Samhain?"

"I'll go anywhere you are, Sunshine."

eighteen
ada

The next week flies by, and Ulgan and I still can't get enough of each other.

He's been staying at my cottage every night after we both agreed that waking up without each other wasn't an option. As much as this small cottage means to me, it really is *small*. My poor mate would never complain, but it has to be uncomfortable trying to squeeze his much larger body into a house that's clearly not made for him. We need to start looking at places soon so we can have a home that's perfect for both of us.

Tonight's festivities will be our first real outing since I accepted that Ulgan and I are mates. It's time to get ready to show him off.

Halloween has always been my favorite holiday. The mysterious and spooky atmosphere draws me in like a moth's endless pursuit to a flame. The idea that you can become whoever you want with a simple costume is endlessly enticing, and the delicious holiday treats make my mouth water just thinking about them. I have a sweet tooth, and I won't lie,

Halloween and candy have always gone together in my mind. It wasn't until I started spending more time with the coven that I learned about the deep history behind Samhain and the different ways that witches celebrate and honor this time of year.

The coven hosts a Dumb Supper that anyone willing to learn about their traditions can attend. I look forward to it every year, but I didn't know what to expect the first time I participated. Rue gave me some idea of what would happen, but there's nothing like experiencing it first hand. Tonight's Dumb Supper is something that I've been counting down the days to, because I have a surprise for Ulgan that I hope he will like.

Ulgan has never attended a coven event before. I decided to treat myself to a new dress for the occasion: a black A-line beauty with sheer billowing black sleeves and sparkling applique stars. The stars shimmer with each movement I make, giving the dress a celestial vibe.

"Ada, would you mind helping me with my cufflinks?" Ulgan calls from the bathroom. He walks out adjusting the sleeve of his well fitted black dress shirt.

Damn, my man cleans up well. It makes me wish we were staying in tonight so I could peel it off of him. Finally breaking out of my sex-crazed stupor, I notice him staring at me, eyes reflecting the hunger in my own.

Oh, I'm taking advantage of this. Sashaying over to him, I do an innocent twirl and ask, "Do you like my dress?" I bat my eyelashes.

A low growl emanates from him, and his hands clench at his sides. "You're playing a dangerous game, Sunshine. Don't start something that you know we can't finish right now." His eyes fixate on the bodice of my dress, which is displaying an obscene amount of cleavage. I knew he'd love it.

"All right, all right. We better hurry up so we aren't late for the welcome. Rue will kill me if I miss it," I say, giggling and giving him a little wink.

WALKING up the path to Blackwood Estate, there's something electric in the air. By the look of awe on Ulgan's face, I don't think he was expecting how grand the affair would be. The drive leading up the estate is now lined with enchanted jack-o-lanterns that hover above the ground and radiate a soft glow. Leaves in every shade of red, yellow, and orange gently fall from the sky and usher guests forward to the house.

The Blackwood coven welcomes guests with a warm reception. Ulgan and I chat with the coven members that I've gotten to know over the years until the front door of the estate opens wide. A hush falls over the crowd.

Angeline and Rue appear and stand on the front steps.

"Hello, everyone," Angeline begins. "My daughter, Rue, and I could not be more thrilled to wish each and every one of you a blessed Samhain. To our honored guests, thank you for attending and joining us for this special evening. Samhain is the time of year where the veil is at its thinnest. This is a time to celebrate and honor our departed loved ones, and one way that we'll do so tonight is with a Dumb Supper. For those of you in attendance for the first time, a Dumb Supper is a silent dinner service where we leave a place at the table for those who are no longer with us physically, but they are certainly here guiding us."

Ulgan and I make our way to one of the many round

tables scattered on the front lawn. The sun has set now and multiple bonfires are lit to provide light and warmth. We find our assigned table, and now I'm also in awe, even though I helped create the decorations for the tablescapes. Each table is covered in a black table cloth and a rich orange runner. A bowl in the centerpiece is filled with acorns, apples, miniature gourds, and cinnamon sticks. Intention candles, oils, and herbs have been placed in small decorative bowls for us to light later this evening. An antique golden lantern floats elegantly above the table, adding an ethereal glow.

I see Ulgan wiping away a tear, and it's clear that he saw my surprise for him this evening. There are place settings at our small table for Ulgan and myself, but there are also place settings for my parents, granny, and the new addition this year: Ulgan's grandmother who passed two years ago. Framed photos of them had been placed at each place setting.

"Did you do this?" he whispers.

"She deserves to be honored this evening, too," I say, my voice trembling with emotion.

"Nana would have loved you." He pulls me in for a brief hug and kiss on the top of my head.

We take our seats, and silence falls over the gathering. Bountiful dishes of roasted chicken and root vegetables, soup, apple tarts, and elaborately decorated cookies in the shape of skeletons and ghosts magically appear on each table. Large pitchers of mead and spiced cider also materialized from thin air. The heavenly scents of the food waft through the air, enveloping the celebration.

Everyone eats in silence for the entirety of the dinner. The only sounds that can be heard are the clinking of silverware against plates, the crackle of the fires, and the occasional creature walking through the forest surrounding the property.

After dinner, everyone crowds around the main bonfire to continue celebrating. Music floats through the party as everyone gets a bit more rowdy, having fun ringing in the witch's new year.

Rue and I dance around the bonfire, our yearly tradition, as Ulgan drinks mead and talks with a few men that he knows from school. As the night winds down, Ulgan and I return to our table to dress and light our intention candles for the upcoming year.

"Am I doing this correctly?" he asks.

"There is no right or wrong way to do this. Rue says it's all in the intentions that you put behind it. Once we light them, our intentions will be declared."

Closing my eyes, I set the intention to continue working to heal from my past, and for abundance for both myself and Ulgan.

Ulgan's eyes are closed, and a grin pulls at the corner of his lips. His brilliant warm brown eyes open and land on me, making me tingle all over.

I love this handsome orc so much.

We say our goodbyes and head home. On the short drive to my cottage, we remain silent until we finally pull into the drive and park. Outside the car, we stand together in the driveway.

"Thank you for including me tonight, Sunshine. That was a beautiful evening, and the fact you thought to include my grandmother means the world to me," he says, pulling me toward him. "I love you so much, mate."

My arms wrap around his neck, running my fingers through the hair near his nape. "I love you, too, my mate." His breath always hitches whenever I call him my mate. It's so damn fun to get him worked up like this.

A low growl rumbles from him. "Mmmm, you know how

much I love hearing you call me that. Now, let's get inside so I can strip you naked and make you scream my name. We don't want to give your neighbors a show. You're all mine." The gravel in his voice has moisture pooling between my thighs, combined with the smolder in his eyes, any woman would melt.

"Now, you know what it does to me when you get all possessive like that. Bring me inside, orc daddy, and have your way with me," I say, teasing him.

He rolls his eyes at me. "All right, let's get going before you come up with an even worse nickname." He bends down slightly and lifts me into his arms, bridal style. It just does something to me when he carries me around like this. I'm almost positive that every woman gets a small thrill from being held like this by a sexy man.

"Get going. I've been dying for your cock since we left the house earlier today." I'm feeling a little bratty tonight, and I know just the orc to take care of me.

I could almost cry with happiness at the life that Ulgan and I are building with each other. Someone pinch me, how is this real?

nineteen
ada

The early morning sun filters into our bedroom, waking me up from a wonderful night's sleep. I've been having the best sleep of my life now that Ulgan is next to me. My eyes are still closed as I roll over to snuggle up to his warmth.

My hand searches his side of the bed, which is empty and cold. Eyes shooting open, I search around the room for him. That's bizarre. Where could he be? My sweet mate typically insists on staying in bed for a few extra minutes each morning so that we can cuddle. He's even asked Benji to start opening the bakery in the morning so he and I can spend more time together.

Then I notice a note on Ulgan's pillow, written in his surprisingly beautiful handwriting.

Good morning Sunshine,

Theo called me this morning and needs help picking up some antiques from a seller in the city. I won't be back until later tonight. I love you, my beautiful Ada.

Love,

Your mate

P.S. I owe you extra time tomorrow for our early morning cuddles.

This certainly solves my missing mate mystery. I smile as I reread his note. It's sometimes hard to believe that someone like Ulgan actually exists. He never misses an opportunity to let me know how much he loves me.

I guess I should probably get out of bed and start my day. Rue and Angeline texted me last night to ask if I could stop by their place for breakfast. I'm actually thrilled that they asked me over since I need advice from Rue about something a bit personal.

My walk to the Blackwood Estate is quick, and before I know it I'm standing outside the house. Hecate appears at my side and winds her way through my legs, rubbing up against me. "Hey there, sweetie." I give her a brief scratch behind the ears then open the front door to find Rue and Angeline lounging in the sitting room.

"Thank Goddess you're here. I just might be dying from starvation." Rue dramatically sprawls out on the couch and fans herself. Angeline and I both roll our eyes and laugh.

"Oh knock it off, you're fine," Angeline playful scolds Rue.

The three of us head to the kitchen where breakfast is neatly set. A large pitcher of orange juice, platter of muffins, and a bowl of fruit salad fill the table.

"Ada, I was thinking a veggie frittata would be wonderful this morning. What do you think?" Angeline asks me as we take our seats.

"That sounds delicious." Angeline is an incredible cook so this is going to be one kickass breakfast. She gracefully walks over to the oven and pulls out a steaming dish that smells heavenly.

After placing the dish on the table, we help ourselves to big heaping portions. A bottle of hot sauce appears in front of Rue. We each add a generous amount to our plates and dig in.

"So, babe, how's life with your big green hunk?" Rue asks, a wicked gleam in her eyes.

Just then, Angeline's cell phone rings, and she walks away to answer. I'm saved by the bell, or I guess saved by the ringtone. "Hello? Okay, slow down. You've got to be kidding me. I'll be right there." Angeline pinches the bridge of her nose in frustration.

"Everything okay over there, Mom?" Rue asks with concern.

"Everything is fine, honey. One of the wards around the property needs a bit of mending. Nothing to worry about. You two enjoy your breakfast." She begins to leave the room.

"I can come too if you need help." Rue offers, pushing her chair back from the table and standing with a smile on her face. I notice the hint of hope in her voice that Angeline would actually take her up on the offer.

"No. No, you and Ada enjoy your breakfast. I'll be fine without help." Rue slumps back in her chair at her mother's dismissal. Her earlier smile has now vanished.

After Angeline leaves, I stand behind Rue and wrap my arms around her. "You okay?" I ask.

Rue's hands are shaking in her lap, and her head leans back

to rest on me. "I just need to stop trying and accept that I'll never be good enough to her." The pain cuts through Rue's words. It kills me to see her like this.

I let go of her and pull Rue up to her feet. "Rue, you listen to me right now. You're *more* than enough. You are Rue-motherfucking-Blackwood, the baddest witch that's ever existed. You care deeply and fiercely for everyone in your life. I love your mom, but if she can't see how talented you are, then that's her loss."

Rue pulls me in for a tight hug and a kiss on the cheek. "I love you, you know that, right?"

"Of course! I love you, too. Now, I have something kind of personal to talk with you about, and I know that embarrassing things bring you happiness," I tease.

"You know me so well," she replies with a laugh. "How about we take this food to my room?"

We fill a tray with food and drinks and make our way upstairs. "Spill. I want every gory detail," Rue says, cutting right to the point as we sit down at the small table in the corner of the room.

"I need to talk about babies," I blurt. So much for trying to ease into this conversation.

"Babies? What the fuck do you think I know about babies?" She narrows her eyes, sounding confused.

"All right, I need you to not tease me about this. Ulgan and I are obviously intimate now that we're together," I say. Rue nods, listening. "The next step for us is to officially go through with our bonding ceremony." I stop, unsure of how to voice what my real worry is.

"Are you having second thoughts about Ulgan?" Rue asks, reaching across the table to hold my hand.

"*No!* No, I'm not having second thoughts. I love him more

than anything. It's just..." I hesitate, feeling embarrassed. "Bonding ceremonies involve knotting, and knotting equals pregnancy. You know that I want to be a mom one day, but not right now." It feels incredible to get that off my chest.

"This is really weighing on you, huh?" she asks.

"Yeah, it is. I want to start a family with Ulgan, but not right now. A knot would guarantee that I become pregnant immediately. Rue, I want to officially be his mate more than anything, but I don't know what to do."

"Have you talked to him about this?" Rue asks, leaning back in her chair.

"I know he's supportive of my choices, but I would feel better if I knew that I had some options to share with him. Have you heard of anything that he and I could do to prevent pregnancy right now?" My mate would never pressure me into anything, and will respect me and my decision.

"Come with me. I think I might have just the thing you need." She pulls me out of my seat and leads me over to the door that connects her bedroom with her "witchy room", as I call it.

Her witchy room is right out of a movie. It's covered from floor to ceiling with different types of plants, piles of spellbooks scattered around, crystals of various colors and sizes, and small glass vials of *who knows what.*

Rue lets go of my hand and approaches a shelf across the room, returning with two medium sized glass vials, one with a vibrant pink liquid and the other a shimmering teal. "I was reading one of the ancient healer spell books in our coven collection a few months ago and came across a potion that my grandmother would make ages ago for anyone in Whispering Springs in an interspecies relationship. Of course, I just had to give it a try and make it myself."

Rue never ceases to amaze me.

She holds up the pink vial and hands it to me. "This potion will prevent pregnancy," she gives me the teal vial, "and this one will reverse the pink potion and allow you to become pregnant. Consider the pink one magical birth control that you only have to take once, and will stop you from getting pregnant from *any* species of monster. The teal vial will immediately reverse the potion, so you and lover boy can start that sweet family of yours when you're ready." Rue tries to be nonchalant about this, but she deserves to be proud of herself. She makes her magic look effortless.

"Rue, you effing genius! This is perfect! I can't wait to see Ulgan tonight and tell him." I give her a big kiss on the cheek. She always knows just what to do.

"Now that we've settled that, how about we head into town and have some retail therapy? And maybe a manicure. We deserve to treat ourselves today."

Shopping with my bestie always ends in us buying way too much crap we don't need and eating way too much yummy food. This sounds like the perfect way to spend the day. I send a quick message to Ulgan letting him know not to expect me home until later, and we head out.

Hours later, I'm walking up to my cottage with my arms loaded with shopping bags. My stomach still hurts from the amount of laughing that Rue and I did today.

That's strange. Ulgan's car is parked outside, but all of the lights in the cottage are off.

"Babe, are you here?" I put the shopping bags down by the door and walk further into the house to find my mate. I search the house and come up empty handed. Where on earth is he?

It's only as I make my way to the kitchen that I can see lights illuminating the backyard through the sliding glass door.

Sliding the door open, I step outside into the backyard to see twinkling lights hanging from the trees, making my little backyard sparkle like I was walking among the stars. Music suddenly starts, and I quickly recognize the tune. *Islands in the Stream* begins and I know that Ulgan has something to do with it. He knows how much this song means to me and how ever since I was a little girl, I hoped that it'd be the song I danced to with my future husband.

"You absolutely wonderful man, you better get out here right now before I start crying."

"I thought you might like this."Ulgan's deep soothing voice comes from behind me.

I lied. The tears are coming regardless. "You did all of this?" I say, looking around in wonder.

"Ada, you deserve the best of everything. This isn't as extravagant as I would've liked for you, but it just seemed like something you'd appreciate."

I brush tears from my eyes. "You know me so well. This is perfect. But what's the occasion?"

"You asked me once why I call you Sunshine." He holds my hands in his and I can feel that they are slightly trembling. "You, Ada, burst into my life like the first glimpse of sun after a rainstorm. You bring so much joy and happiness into the lives of those around you, and I will forever consider myself the luckiest orc in existence that the fates decided that I am worthy of you."

He reaches up to remove his glasses and wipes tears from his eyes. Ulgan's heart is one of the most beautiful parts of him.

"Ada, I want to officially ask you to become my mate, *and* my wife." He lowers himself down to one knee, pulling out a small black ring box from his pocket. "Ada Walker, will you be my mate, and let me love you forever?"

Ulgan's hands shake as he opens the ring box to reveal a beautiful oval cut emerald ring, the large stone flanked by tiny diamonds that sparkle in the moonlight.

Sinking to my knees with him, I throw my arms around Ulgan and kiss him deeply. Oh, I probably should respond to his question. Cupping his face in my hands, both of us have tears running down our faces. "Yes, a million times yes! I love you so much!" We stay like this for a long time, just holding each other and kissing like the world will collapse if we don't.

Ulgan helps me to stand and slides the ring on my finger. "Our bonding ceremony is private and just between us, but we can have a human wedding too if you'd like."

"I don't need a wedding." I just need my big green teddy bear every single day of my life. "Maybe a party or something later, but I like the idea that this is just between you and me."

"We've talked a bit about orc mating rituals. There's one part that I didn't mention, but should have."

He looks unsure of himself, so my arms go around his waist and urge him to go on.

"When an orc finds his mate, he can only officially claim her by triggering a mating heat and experiencing it with that mate."

"Ulgan, I know about the mating heat," I interrupt.

"You do?" His eyes widen in shock.

"Yeah, I may or may not have done a bit of research when we started seeing each other. You're the first orc that I've ever dated, so I wanted to know what to expect." Now probably isn't the best time to mention that my research involved monster romance novels. I'll tell him later.

"Goddess help me not make this more awkward. Are you ready for my knot?" he says, cheeks darkening.

"Oh hell yeah I am, and I'm freaking excited for it." Was that too eager of me? He roars with laughter. "We haven't discussed babies yet, but I think we should. Being a mother has been something I've wanted for ages, but I'm not ready just yet," I share.

One of Ulgan's arms tighten around me, as he raises his other hand to cup my cheek so that I'm looking into his eyes. "Before you panic, orcs have come a long way medically. I've been on suppressants to dampen the mating heat since we met. I will never force you into anything. Yes, I want to be a father, but only when we're both ready. I can continue using the suppressants until that time."

"We have another option." I let go of him and head into the house, returning with the two vials from Rue.

"Option two is that you stop taking the suppressants. Rue gave me a potion today that will allow us to have as much sex as we want without having to worry about having a baby, and this other vial will reverse it so that we can start our family." I show him the vials and he holds them, examining each one.

"So, option two means what exactly?" Once again, he's making sure that I know he'll respect whatever decision I make.

"Option two means that your mating heat will be triggered," I tell him, stepping closer.

"Sunshine, I haven't taken my dose today, so my heat is

starting. We would need to stay here and make love until the heat dies down in a few days. It would mean that my knot would finally lock inside of your sweet pussy, and I would fill you up with my cum over and over again until you are dripping with it."

Holy shit. Copious amounts of sex with nothing between us and no baby until I'm ready? Sign my ass up!

"Option two," I say immediately. "I want option two. Make me officially yours, Ulgan."

His eyes close in what appears to be an effort to get control of himself.

I reach over and take the pink vial from his hand. His eyes pop open and we lock gazes as I uncork it and drink the contents, which surprisingly tastes like strawberries. Yum.

"Goddess save me, Ada. I was hoping that you'd say that. Follow me, little mate." He intertwines our fingers and leads me to the bedroom. I release a gasp as I take the room in.

Where the ceiling used to be, it now appears as if the night sky is overhead, twinkling with stars. "How in the world..." I say, unable to finish my thought.

"This is a bonding gift from Rue. She enchanted the ceiling to mirror the night sky. It's an old orc tradition that mated pairs would consummate their bond in the fresh air under the stars." My bestie is the best. My heart could burst with my love for her.

"I love you with everything that I am, Ulgan."

"You, Ada, have turned my life upside down in the best way. You were always meant to be mine, and I meant to be yours. I love you, Sunshine."

Slowly, he makes his way to me. I reach for the hem of my sweater, but Ulgan is faster. His hands brushing mine away. "You are my present to unwrap, mate." His hands replace mine and he eases the soft sweater over my head until it falls to the floor.

"I need to feel you." Desperation to touch him and be touched by him, needing to see him, takes over me. My fingers begin unbuttoning his dress shirt, making quick work of the buttons. Easing the shirt off his shoulders and giving myself plenty of time to feel him up.

"Are you enjoying yourself?" he laughs. Looping my thumbs into the waistband of his pants I pull him toward me.

"Very, very much." Leaning toward him, I duck my head and place kisses across his broad chest.

Ulgan gives a sigh of contentment. My tongue traces the black swirling design that is hard to keep my hands and tongue off of. His tattoos are a work of art. He shared with me that the tattoos are a traditional orcish design that ancient orc warriors would cover their bodies with. I desperately need to sketch the historic pattern.

"That little tongue of yours is dangerous, mate." His hands travel up my back to the clasp of my bra. He undoes it with ease, and I move back just enough for it to fall to the floor. My hard nipples catch Ulgan's attention and he plays with one while sucking the other into his mouth.

"That feels so good, baby." My words cut off on a moan, as his tongue swirls around the overly sensitive peak, and he gives it one final intense suck before releasing it with a pop. He moves on to the other. My nails score his back as I hold on to him for dear life, my knees weak.

"Ulgan, I need you." My voice is desperate. His gaze meets with mine and there is something primal in them.

"Sunshine, I can feel the mating heat taking over. Are you sure that this is what you want?" He gives me one more chance to change my mind, but I'll be damned if I'm leaving now.

"I want you, my mate. Make love to me. I am one hundred percent in love with you, and I always will be. Now, get your ass out of those pants and get on that bed so I can have my wicked way with you."

He smirks and complies with my request. As he shucks off his pants and briefs, I quickly remove my clothes. Both naked now, I push him back on the bed and climb onto his lap, sitting up so I can memorize every inch of his muscular body. It will never get old seeing the look of love on his face. Bending down, I capture his lips with mine and he quickly takes control of the kiss. His lips work mine and his tongue tastes my bottom lip until I open for him. Our tongues move against each other and the room fills with the sounds of our heavy breaths and moans.

Ulgan's hands reach around to hold onto my ass, bringing my hips down to rub against his hard cock. Placing my hands on his chest for support, I eagerly move my hips to create more friction. Holy crap, if his cock isn't inside of me soon I just may combust. "Ulgan, I need you inside of me."

In one smooth motion he flips us so I'm underneath him on my back. His eyes are filled with heat as he captures my mouth in a rough kiss. Well, this is new and I'm low key loving it.

"Not yet, little mate. I need to prepare you for my knot." One arm supports his weight above me while the other snakes between my legs and touches my core. "You're so wet for me already. Are you trying to drive me crazy?" His index finger runs through my slit before playing around my center.

My breath hitches as he inserts a finger into me. He slowly removes it and then thrusts it back in. A scream is ripped from me. This man's fingers are national damn treasures.

Slowly torturing my pussy, Ulgan inserts another finger, and I can feel myself stretching with each thrust as I ride his hand. Just when an orgasm is within reach, he inserts a third finger and I shatter. My head falls back on the soft pillow, and the stars seem to shimmer above me.

Ulgan works inside of me until my orgasm dies down. Then, the smug bastard shoots me a satisfied glance before removing his fingers and holding them to his mouth, glistening. He slowly licks each finger clean with that big tongue of his. "You taste so good, love, but I'm going to need a lot more. Your body is my new favorite dessert."

Working his way down my body he places kisses on every bit of skin he can reach. I thoroughly enjoy seeing this man between my legs.

Ulgan eases my legs apart, making space for his large body. "Mmmm," he groans, gently kissing my inner thighs and then a final kiss to my core. A shiver runs through me, and then I feel his tongue lick straight through my slick slit. He laps at my pussy, moaning with each pass of his rough tongue. Without warning, he stiffens his tongue and begins to thrust it deep inside of me. His thumb strokes my clit until all I can see are those twinkling stars again as my body falls apart.

"You taste like perfection. I could spend hours between your thighs, and one day I will." He continues licking until he's drunk down every last drop. "Do you think you're ready for me? Are you going to be a good little mate and let me fuck you now?" His dirty mouth gets me even more wet.

"Please, please fuck me, Ulgan. I need to feel you inside of me. Don't make me wait any longer." If he doesn't do it soon I'm flipping us and taking over.

"You've waited long enough, my love. Are you ready for my knot? During the frenzy, this part of me will swell and lock us together." He leans over me again, gripping his knot that's already starting to expand. "Don't panic, it will go down eventually, but soon after I'll need to be inside of you again."

"Do you see me complaining? It aches so much right now. Please, I need you."

Ulgan lines himself up with my core and slowly the head of his cock breaches my entrance. This is a familiar feeling now, but it gets better each time. Ulgan slowly enters me until his knot bumps against my pussy. Rising above me, his arms keep his weight off me as his hips pick up speed and he thrusts in and out.

"You feel so damn good inside of me," I moan. "Give me your knot, baby. I need more." I match his rhythm as he slams his hips into me, as his knot rubs against my entrance. He continues to tease me, not giving me what I want just yet.

"Ulgan, now!" He pounds into me over and over. Then, he gives one final deep thrust and my body feels indescribably full. The breath leaves my body and my mouth opens in a silent scream. Ulgan continues to rock into me as my channel spasms around him as I come. Seconds later, he shouts my name and his cock unleashes what feels like an endless stream of cum. He keeps his arms locked to keep himself from crushing me as he shoots his final load deep into me.

His arms give out and he collapses. The feeling of his weight on top of me feels wonderful and I hold him in my arms as his head rests in the crook of my neck. Both of our bodies are sweaty and sticky and we lie like this for a while until his knot goes down and he's able to slide out of me, causing a mixture of both of us to drip down onto the bed. He rolls to lay on his back. We rest like this for a few minutes, catching our breath and looking up at the stars.

"Ada?" he asks.

I turn my head and find him already staring at me like I'm the most precious thing in the world to him. "Yes?"

"I'm so thankful I found you."

"Come here, you sweet man." He bends down so I can kiss him, trying to pour all of my love for him into it. "You're more than I could've ever dreamed of. Are we officially mates now?"

He brushes my bangs away from my damp forehead and places a kiss there. "Yes, my beautiful mate. It's official now."

"Are you ready for round two?" Reaching down to cup one of my breasts, I give it a little squeeze. "I need you again," I pout.

"You're insatiable. Let me take care of you, Sunshine," he growls, then dives at me. I let out a laugh, but it quickly turns to a moan. My mate knows just what I want.

twenty
ulgan

"Ulgan, can you grab the charcuterie board from the fridge and bring it out to the car?" Ada calls from the front door, arms filled with bouquets of flowers for my mom, Selene, and Miss Laurel. I picked up Miss Laurel last week and she's been staying with my mom at her house. My thoughtful mate decided that all of the ladies in my family deserve some fresh blooms.

"What is it with you humans and cheese boards?"

"Don't you dare speak negatively about charcuterie boards," Ada chastises me.

Ada has been teaching me about the beauty and art of making a proper charcuterie board. I still don't see the appeal, but if it makes my love happy to put a bunch of stuff on a wooden tray, then I'll be there each time to cheer her on and devour it.

"I promise to never disparage the almighty charcuterie again. I'll bring it right outside. Do you need any help getting these flowers to the car?" I ask, holding out my arms.

"Thank you, my handsome mate, but I'm all set over here.

You've got yourself an independent woman." She balances the bouquets in one arm and raises her other to flex her bicep.

The past few weeks have felt like walking in a daydream. Ada and I have fallen into a daily routine that brings me such contentment and joy. Each day I get to wake up next to the most beautiful woman in the world, and at night we come back together to support one another, laugh, and make love.

I grab what we need from the fridge, and head outside. I place everything in the back of my Jeep, and then walk around to the drivers side to hop in. Ada is already in the passenger seat, which she calls her passenger princess throne. I don't know where she comes up with this shit, but it certainly keeps me on my toes.

We drive the short distance to my mother's house, where we're meeting everyone for an early dinner. We've only just parked in the driveway when Selene comes bursting out of the house, hurrying over to the car.

"Hey," I open my door and call out to her. "Mind helping us bring all of this inside?"

Selene ignores me and goes right over to Ada. The two of them hug and begin talking excitedly. Seeing my mate and sister get along so well is a relief.

"Ada, you will not believe who Mom invited to dinner tonight!" Selene is buzzing. Someone's joining us today?

"Who did Mom invite? Hello, by the way," I say, pulling her in for a brief hug.

"Hey, big bro. Mom has a guy over!" It takes me a second to process this. Ada and Selene both squeal with delight. My mother hasn't dated anyone to my knowledge since her mate died, way before she adopted Selene and I. Who is this mystery man and what are his intentions with my mother?

"Come inside and meet him," Selene says. "He's actually a really great guy."

That puts me at ease, at least. We unload the car and enter the house. I spot Miss Laurel first and she slowly gets up from her chair to give Ada and I hugs, her vines wrapping around each of us.

Mom's voice calls from the kitchen. "Is that my Ulgie and Ada? Come in here you two. I have someone I want you to meet."

As if she could sense my trepidation, Ada holds my hand, giving it a squeeze. We find my mom in the kitchen chopping vegetables on the island, and an older cyclops with graying hair and a mustache sits across from her on a stool, folding napkins into different animals.

"Oh those are so freaking cool!" Ada lights up with excitement. "I'm Ada, and this is my mate, Ulgan. Can you teach me how to make those?"

I guess her love for art extends to napkins, too.

"Ada and Ulgan, I want you to meet my friend, Harold. Harold, this is my son Ulgan and his adorable mate, Ada." My mother beams as she introduces us.

"It's nice to meet you, Harold," I say, extending my hand to shake his. Ada always says that she can tell if someone is a good person by looking at their eyes. She swears that good people have kind eyes. Well, Harold only has one, but it's clear to see how much he cares for Mom, because he can't take that eye off of her when she's talking.

"It's great to meet you both. Edie's been telling me all about you. Thank you for letting me crash your family dinner."

Selene enters the kitchen, her arm is wrapped around Miss Laurel to keep her stable, and guides her to sit at the new table that I finished just last week.

"All right, now that all of the niceties are out of the way, somebody bring that cheese and crackers over here. I'm effing starving." Miss Laurel is infamous around here for being hangry.

Sitting at the table with Selene and Miss Laurel, I watch Harold teach Ada the art of napkin folding, which he shares he learned while working at one of the top restaurants in the city. Ada runs over to show me the napkin bunny she's made. Her enthusiasm for life is contagious.

All of the food is ready, and I help Mom to place all of the warm dishes on the table. The aroma has my mouth watering. Everyone takes their seat and digs in. It doesn't escape my notice that Harold is serving Mom first before getting his portion. That certainly wins him some points with me. Ada's arm is draped over the back of my chair and she's lazily rubbing my back. Her touch grounds me.

"Ada, darling, you must join my book club next week for our monthly meeting." Mom's book club, the NecROMANCERS, read all kinds of alien and monster smut. My mother is a bit too open about what she reads, which means I've heard far too much about aliens with multiple dicks and monsters with tentacles.

"I would love to! What are you reading this month?" Goddess, help me.

"There's this wonderful author named Ivy Knox that writes the most delicious books. We're currently reading her series about dragon alien shifter brothers that have landed on Earth. The male lead is so yummy."

No man should have to hear his own mother call another man "yummy".

"Say less, you had me at dragon alien shifters." Ada has shared her book collection with me, so it comes as no surprise that this kind of book would be right up her alley. Just the other night she was trying to explain why she has a 'feral love' for a series by an author named Hazel Mack. According to Ada, the series is about a town kind of like Whispering Springs where monsters live, but as Ada put it, "That is one small town I wouldn't mind visiting, if ya know what I mean. Everyone is freaking gorgeous!"

The dinner winds down, and the ladies go to the living room to relax while Harold and I wash the dishes.

"There is nothing sexier than a man washing dishes." Ada winks at me and pinches my ass, making sure that no one else saw.

Whispering into her ear, I growl, "You're going to pay for that later, little mate."

"Can't wait!" She gives me another wink before sauntering off to the living room, giving me a show by swaying her hips in the way that I like. That lucious woman is a handful, and I wouldn't change a thing about her.

After Harold and I finish up, we join everyone else in the living room. Ada moves over on the couch to make room for me. I sit down and without warning, Selene bombards me with questions.

"Ada was just telling us that you're both thinking about planning a party to celebrate your mating ceremony. I would love to volunteer my event planning services." I should've known that Selene would be all over planning this party, and to be honest, I'm quite thankful. Party planning isn't something I've ever had to do, so I have no clue where to start.

"Does this mean that you'll be staying in town?" Ada asks, trying to keep her excitement in check.

"I figured Whispering Springs could use an event planner, so yes, I'm staying."

"I've missed having you around, Selene. It will be awesome to have you living close by." The news gives me a sense of contentment.

"Yes! This is the best news ever! Rue, Isla, and Hannah are going to freak when they find out!" Ada runs over to give her a hug, and then joins me back on the couch.

"Honey, I'm so happy to hear that we'll be seeing more of you." Mom has unshed tears in her eyes.

Looking at the clock, it's time for me to show Ada her surprise. Everybody else at the dinner was already in on my plans, so hopefully this will go smoothly.

"Okay, everyone. I have a surprise that I need to show Ada, so we'll be leaving now." I probably could've been more eloquent in my announcement, but I'm just too excited to care.

Ada shoots me a confused look, but decides to go along with it once she sees how excited everyone else in the room is. She hugs everyone and promises to call Selene the next day to meet up for lunch to discuss the party.

Hurrying Ada into my Jeep, we head toward our destination.

"Baby, where are we going? You know that surprises make me nervous." That I do. I rest my hand on her thigh like always and rub my thumb in soothing circles.

"This is a good surprise, I promise." My hands are shaking lightly, a mix of nervous energy and excitement.

We finally reach our destination, and Ada shoots me a confused look as I put the car in park and go around to open her door for her.

"Ulgan, what am I looking at?" she asks, still trying to piece together the puzzle.

Before us is a two story white Cape Cod style home with a spacious front porch, gabled roof, and large windows that will let in a good amount of natural sunlight.

Ada is standing in front of me, and I can't stop myself from wrapping my arms around her waist and resting my chin on her shoulder. "The house is ours, Sunshine. Do you like it?" I ask, whispering into her ear and kissing her cheek. A lump forms in my throat as I wait for her to respond.

"Wait a minute. This house is ours? How is that possible?" She turns to face me. Astonishment is written all over her lovely face.

"I worked with Declan to design the house, and helped his crew to build it whenever I had free time," I say with pride.

"When the hell did you have time to do all of this?" she asks, confused still.

"Sunshine, we've been working on this since the day we drove over to see Miss Laurel. If I'm being honest, Declan's crew did most of the work. Maybe it was a bit presumptuous of me to do this, but it helped to give me hope. Hoping that one day you and I would be together and live here." I will do anything to make this woman happy. "Could you see yourself living here?"

"This is real, isn't it? You actually built my dream house. Oh, Ulgan, this is incredible." She jumps up, wrapping her arms around my neck. I spin her around and allow her laughter to envelop me. "Can we go inside?" she asks, once I've set her down.

"This is your house, Sunshine. You can see anything you like. The inside isn't finished just yet, but I want you to be included in all of those decisions. Can I recommend that you start at your art studio on the second floor? It has a great view of the spring."

"You made me a freaking art studio!" Ada grabs my hand and

drags me into our home. "Holy shit, you're totally getting laid tonight."

Taking a page from Ada's favorite books, this orc is ready for his happily ever after with his Sunshine.

twenty-one
ada

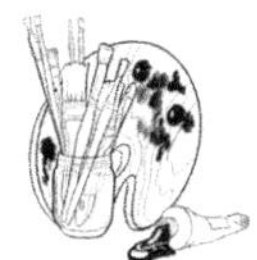

Our bonding party is in full swing at the Blackwood Estate. Rue and her mom insisted on hosting the event, and just as I predicted, Selene hit it off with them. She helped organize everything, and she's even in talks to help plan the coven's Sabbat celebrations from now on.

Selene is the first person to grab me and pull me in for a hug once Ulgan and I arrive at the party. She and I have become closer since we met at Ulgan's apartment. Joining my little girl gang of misfits, she's become one of my closest friends. She's even been helping me decorate the new house, and *boy* does she have excellent taste.

Now that Ulgan and I have moved into our new home, Selene has thankfully agreed to take over the lease for my cottage. It still seems unreal that he helped build a whole ass house for me. The art studio is probably my favorite room. Well, besides the bedroom. The studio has beautiful large windows that let in just the right amount of natural light for painting. Ulgan even built me a custom table and cabinets so that I have plenty of space to create and store supplies. He's so thoughtful to have given me such a generous surprise. He's yet to let me paint a portrait of him naked, but I think I'm wearing him down.

The inside of the sprawling estate is decorated—and enchanted—with hundreds of thousands of flowers that hang from the ceiling and can be found on every available surface. It feels like we're in a whimsical garden surrounded by those who Ulgan and I love dearly. Everyone is scattered throughout the room eating the almost-too-pretty-to-eat hors d'oeuvres and chatting happily.

Ulgan and I make our way around the room, thanking everyone for coming and celebrating us. It doesn't escape my notice that Theo has some difficulty keeping his eyes off of Rue today. There's something there that I just can't put my finger on.

Isla and Hannah are both having an animated conversation with Miss Laurel as Kaida zooms around the room twirling in her new flowy dress. Everyone I love is under one roof.

Out of the corner of my eye, I see Sebastian walking toward us, flanked by some familiar faces.

"Ada, you look like an absolute babe today!" Clio rushes at me, giving me a big hug. Her fiery curls pop in contrast with the deep green dress that she's chosen. Sarah isn't far behind, wrapping her arms around me next. My coworker always looks elegant, and this floral romper she's got on is perfection.

"Ada, this party is gorgeous. Congratulations to you and Ulgan. I'm so happy for you." She gives both Ulgan and I a warm smile. Sarah looks behind her, and grabs the hand of a large giant of a man. "Max, this is my friend Ada that I've been telling you about, and her new mate Ulgan. Ulgan, Ada, this is my mate, Max."

Max looks lovingly at Sarah before turning his gaze to us,

wishing Ulgan and I a wonderful life together. His gaze travels back to Sarah, where he looks at her like she hung the moon.

"Brother, get over here and congratulate them!" Sarah turns to Sebastian, tugging him forward.

Wait, Sarah and Sebastian are related? I know that they belong to the same pack, but I certainly didn't know that they are siblings.

"Brother?" I quietly whisper to her.

"Oh yeah, did I forget to mention that? This grumpy ass has been blessed to call me his sister."

"Blessed? More like cursed," Sebastian mutters under his breath, clearly amused. So, Sebastian is related to both Clio and Sarah. Those girls sure have some explaining to do at our weekly dinner later this week.

Sebastian is dapper in a gray suit, something that he looks incredibly uncomfortable in, as he pulls at his tie. He and the high ranking members of his pack are here to represent the shifter community.

"Congratulations to the happy couple. I hope y'all have many years of happiness ahead of you. On behalf of the Artemis Pack, we hope that you'll accept these gifts, and also take my thanks. We wolf shifters aren't always included in events like this, so it means a lot to my people. You will have the gratitude and protection of the pack for as long as I'm alpha." Sebastian hands Ulgan a large basket overflowing with handmade soaps, candles, and jams, made by members of his pack. The pack is known for their unique locally sourced artisan goods.

Big tears pour down my face. "Sebastian, get over here so that I can hug you!"

His entire body stiffens as I wrap my arms around him, but eventually he relaxes and returns my hug.

Releasing Sebastian, I address all of the shifters standing behind him. "Please enjoy the party, and I am so excited to get to know you and your mates." Each of the men gives me a smile and goes off to enjoy themselves. Sarah and Clio each give me a wave and join their pack mates.

Suddenly, Theo appears beside Ulgan, buzzing with excitement. "Hey man, you won't believe who I just ran into. Stefan from high school! Come with me and say hi." Ulgan appears excited to hear that an old friend is able to be here today.

"Ada, is it okay if I borrow your mate for a few minutes?" Theo asks. I swear, sometimes they act like two little boys when they're together.

"Yes, Ulgan may come out to play." We all laugh.

"Thanks, Ada! I'll be sure to have him back by curfew." Theo gives me a wink. They walk outside and I can hear their cheers of excitement even over the sounds of the loud party.

"Ada, you look stunning, sweetheart." Angeline comes up beside me and wraps me in a hug, then holds me at arms length to take in my dress. All of the ladies in my life went with me to pick out this sweet floor length blue dress with lantern sleeves and beautiful floral embroidery that matches the flowers surrounding us. "You are my second daughter, and to see you this happy and in love is the best gift anyone could ask for. I'm so happy for you."

After stepping in as a surrogate mom, I don't think I will ever be able to repay her. "I love you, Angeline."

Edie and Harold make their way over to us. "Angeline you have outdone yourself. Thank you for everything you've done for my boy and Ada. This whole place looks like a floral dream." Harold nods enthusiastically while keeping his hand on Edie's back. Those two are so damn cute.

"Your Selene and my Rue are to thank for all of this. It was their idea to bring spring a few months early," Angeline replies. "That Selene is a powerhouse that I look forward to working with again, and for our families to get to know each other better."

"Hi, Sunshine," Ulgan whispers in my ear from behind me.

"There you are. Did you have fun with your friends?" I've grossed myself out with how much I missed him in the short time that we weren't together.

"Yes, I did, but I missed my mate. I have one more surprise for you, if you're ready."

What could he possibly surprise me with now? Is he gonna bring out a new car or something?

Ulgan clears his throat, and the room becomes quiet. "Hello, everyone. Ada and I want to thank all of you for coming today to celebrate our mating bond. There is one final surprise that I have in store for my gorgeous mate. It has come to my attention that as a part of human wedding ceremonies, there's typically a cake that the couple cut together. If you know me, I happen to know my way around cake." The crowd bursts out laughing. He grabs my hands and speaks directly to me, "Ada, I love you with my entire heart. This cake was made by me, with love."

Suddenly, Theo and Sebastian carry out an enormous five tiered cake with round layers and a rainbow of frosting in a variety of pastel colors.

"Ulgan, it's gorgeous," I accidentally shout, in love with the cake and forgetting to use my inside voice.

He chuckles at my reaction, and the rest of the crowd follows suit. "I thought you might like it, since you've never been shy about your love of color."

We walk over and cut out a slice of the cake while the room cheers. We each take a bite of the cake, and I swear that I moan the second it hits my taste buds. Vanilla sponge with lavender and a lemon curd filling.

"Holy shit, Ulgan. This may be my favorite cake you've ever made." The crowd goes back to chatting and having fun, and Ulgan and I are left to spend a few moments alone together.

"I'm glad you like it. You actually inspired the flavor," he said mischievously.

"Really, how so?" I ask curiously.

"Remember how I said that orcs can scent their mates? Well, to me you smell like lavender and lemon."

"Awe, that's sweet." He's such a romantic. "What about the vanilla?"

He leans in close, whispering so only I can hear, "When that delicious body of yours gets aroused and your pussy soaks your panties, there's a touch of vanilla in your scent. It's mouthwatering."

He—what? I slowly blink at him, making sure I heard him correctly. "You made a cake inspired by how I smell when I'm turned on? I can't decide if that's deranged or the sexiest thing that's come out of your mouth."

"Would it help if we snuck away for a few moments so that I can show you what else my mouth can do?" The big goof wiggles his eyebrows up and down at me. I don't need to be asked twice.

My gaze meets his and I see the same heat in his eyes that's working its way through me. "Follow me, I may know just the right place for us to 'freshen up,'" I say, holding up my fingers for air quotes.

"I'll follow you anywhere, my mate."

Hearing him call me his mate will never get old.

twenty-two

rue

"Rue, why aren't you wearing that dress that I chose for you? It would be so much more flattering than what you currently have on."

I fight the urge to roll my eyes at my mother's comment. Angeline Blackwood has been criticizing my appearance since I was a kid, so you'd think I was used to it by now. The familiar sting of her words begins to settle in. Don't get me wrong, I know that my mother loves me, but her disapproval has been something that I wish I didn't need to navigate.

"Thanks Mom, for that helpful feedback," I say, hoping my retort stops her from going further.

"Sweetheart, I'm just trying to be helpful. Here, let me fix your hair."

Now there's apparently an issue with my hair. Screw this, I'm supposed to be having fun at my best friend Ada's bonding party, but here I am being poked and prodded by my mother.

Swatting her hand away from my tight curls, I narrow my eyes in her direction letting her know to drop it. "Mom, I love you.

Let's just have fun. I mean, look at how many people are here to celebrate Ada and Ulgan."

That's right, I'm the queen of deflecting.

My mom loops her arm through mine and gives me a little nudge. "You're right. Our Ada looks so happy, doesn't she?"

Ada has been like a sister to me since we first met in college. I was a sad and lonely witch in a new city, but the Goddess smiled down on me when she brought Ada's sunshiney self into my life.

"Yeah, she looks so damn happy. I'm going to go talk to her. I'll catch up with you later." I lean over to kiss my mom's cheek and walk across the lively party to where Ada is chatting with her new mother-in-law Edie.

"There's my best friend!" Ada shouts, wrapping her arms around me and pulling me in for a hug. Ada always makes me feel happy and seen. Being her friend is easy.

"Here I am! You miss me?" I ask, wiggling my eyebrows up and down to make her laugh.

"Of course I did. I was just telling Edie that I would join her book club next week for their monthly meeting. Want to come?" she asks.

"Is this the same book club that reads about monsters with big dongs and sexy aliens?" Please say yes. Ada and our friend Hannah have me hooked on the smutty books that they read.

"Oh! I love that description of our book club," Edie says excitedly. I remember spending so much time around her when I was a kid. Ulgan, Theo, and I used to be friends when we were young. We'd spend every day after school together, playing and laughing. That all changed right before I left for college. My heart aches just thinking about it, so I decide to shove that feeling deep down to unpack later...or maybe never.

"Rue, we would love to have you join us," Edie says. "I think you'll really enjoy this month's selection. I can stop by The Enchantress later this week so you can borrow my copy and catch up. Plus, I've missed chatting with you. It's been way too long since we've caught up with each other." She gives me a soft smile. I miss our talks probably more than she does. Edie understood the difficult relationship that I have with my mother and always gave me the best advice.

"I'd love that. Maybe we can grab lunch together too?" I ask.

"It's a date, dear." She leans over and gives me a kiss on the cheek. Miss Edie Durzum is one of a kind. A mischievous look crosses her face as she tries to make her voice sound as innocent as possible. "Rue, doesn't Theo look dashing today?" she says, turning her body to face the dance floor where I'm already painfully aware of his presence.

Humoring her, I begrudgingly turn my body to look in the direction that she's pointing. I become lost in the moment, watching the man who I thought I'd have a future with charm everyone around him.

"You should just go and talk to him." I jump and clutch my heart, startled by the sound of Ada's voice in my ear. My apparently stealthy best friend has caught me staring at a certain handsome elf across the room.

Damn Theo for looking so effing good today. Almost the entire town gathered at my family's house today to celebrate Ada and Ulgan finally going through with their bonding ceremony. Those two took their sweet time to realize how perfect they are for each other. Goddess, my heart is ready to burst with happiness seeing the two of them together and so in love. Ada and Ulgan are two of the best people that I know, and deserving of all the support they are receiving today.

"I have no idea what you're talking about." I try to play it cool, running a hand through my tight brown curls.

"Rue, are you really pretending that you haven't had your eyes locked on Theo since he got here?" Ada narrows her eyes at me, pursing her lips. Edie gives me a wink before excusing herself.

I can feel myself becoming flushed as Ada's gaze intensifies. This is all his fault. He's the one who broke my heart all those years ago, and he keeps popping up in my life being all charming and sexy. What an asshole.

"Fine. I was looking at him, but it's only because he's dancing with Miss Laurel, and she looks beautiful today." I refuse to admit that the real reason is because my heart is melting watching him twirl the elderly dryad around the dancefloor. He makes it hard for me to hate him when he goes and does something sweet like that.

"Sure you were." Ada rolls her eyes and gives me a nudge in the side with her elbow. Clearly, I need to work on my lying skills.

As if he can sense I'm looking at him, Theo swiftly locks eyes with me. I don't know if it was a trick of the light, but I swear his typically blue eyes flash violet for a moment.

That's weird. Breaking our eye contact, I shake my head trying to shake the memories of him away like an Etch-a-Sketch. Damn that beautiful elf and his stupid gorgeous face. Turning around, I start to make my way to the refreshment table for a glass of iced tea when a hand gently lands on my shoulder, stopping me in my tracks.

"Rue."

And just like that, my heart pounds in my chest. I'd recognize that voice from across the room, especially since it's been haunting my dreams for years.

Fingers crossed I don't hex his ass for bothering me.

acknowledgments

To my family- You will probably never read this, which I'm totally fine with. Thank you for encouraging my love of writing, and for always telling me, "You should write a book." Little did you know it would be monster smut

Stewie- You were the best furry brother that I could have ever asked for. Thank you for cuddling with me while I wrote, and for being "the handsomest boy in all the land". I love you, Stewboo.

Janieva- Bestie! Thank you for being one of my biggest cheerleaders, and for putting up with me for years. Love you!

Mena, Kayla, & Carlotta- You beautiful freaking souls. Your guidance made this book possible. I cannot thank you enough for encouraging me during this process and for always reminding me to believe in myself.

My beta readers- Thank you for reading my book baby, and giving your feedback. You all helped to make *Her Sweet Orc* the best it could be.

My therapist- You know who you are, and how much I adore you.

Without your guidance, I never would have healed enough to even consider writing a book.

Kit Fox- Words cannot express how much I love this cover. I cannot express how much it means to me to see a truly plus sized woman on the cover of my book.

Ivy Knox & Anna Fury/Hazel Mack- Thank you for sharing your characters with the world. Both of you are two of the kindest humans on the planet, and your books continue to entertain and inspire me. Love you both!

Fantasy Sprite Studio & Rouge Fox Art- Both of you are two of the most talented people I know. You each brought Ada and Ulgan to life with your own unique styles. I will treasure your artwork for the rest of my life.

To anyone that reads *Her Sweet Orc*- You helped make my dreams a reality. There is no way I could possibly express how much it means to me that you read this.

about the author

Meg Rhodes is a New England native that enjoys reading and writing monster smut, making dirty jokes, and finding any excuse to bring up Taylor Swift or Dolly Parton. She has always dreamed of being an author, so the fact that someone is reading this right now is a dream come true.

When she's not living her best life as a homebody, Meg can be found awkwardly dancing in public, singing along to her favorite playlist at the top of her lungs or talking someone's ear off about her love of history.

Meg LOVES to connect with readers and other authors, so be sure to check out her social media!

Email: megrhodesauthor@gmail.com

instagram.com/megrhodes_author

threads.net/@megrhodes_author

Printed in Great Britain
by Amazon